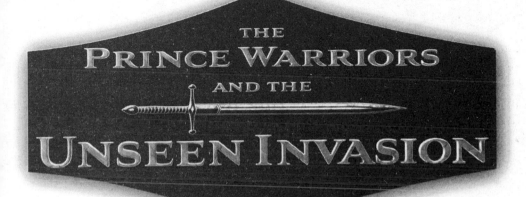

THE

PRINCE WARRIORS

AND THE

UNSEEN INVASION

The Prince Warriors series

Book 1
The Prince Warriors

Book 2
The Prince Warriors and the Unseen Invasion

Book 3
The Prince Warriors and the Swords of Rhema

Book 4
The Winter War

Unseen: The Prince Warriors 365 Devotional

PRISCILLA SHIRER

WITH GINA DETWILER

PUBLISHING GROUP
Nashville,
Tennessee

978-1-0877-4859-7

Published by B&H Publishing Group
Nashville, Tennessee

Dewey Decimal Classification: JF
Subject Heading: COURAGE \ WAR STORIES \ TRUST

1 2 3 4 5 6 • 25 24 23 22 21

For Jerry Jr.
Our second born son.
Our Prince Warrior.

Contents

Prologue

A small figure, clothed in deep purple, skimmed silently across the floor of the vast room. Snakes slithered out of his path, thousands of snakes that littered the floor, hissing and rattling their tails. The figure paused before the throne—a huge sculpture made of greenish iron. It had the shape of a crude tree made of entwined human forms, scrawny legs and arms twisted in bizarre contortions. Behind the throne was a wall of fire, the flames illuminating the agonized faces embedded in the sculpture, making them seem alive.

More writhing snakes carpeted the seat of the throne, their green, iridescent scales gleaming in the firelight. They lashed out with their forked tongues as the figure in the purple robe raised up one draped arm. A hand emerged from the sleeve—pure glowing white—piercing the darkness. The snakes recoiled, deserting the throne, hissing furiously in protest.

The figure lifted the seat of the throne to expose a compartment underneath. He pulled out its contents: a small metal object with four corkscrew crosspieces. A key. He slipped the peculiar key into his purple robe.

The violent hissing of the snakes rose to a fever pitch as the figure turned from the throne and sped away. The faces in the sculpture cried out in a fresh agony.

A huge and horrible shadow rose up from the throne, wielding a massive sword. It crashed down too late—the intruder was already gone.

PART ONE

The Smallest Seed

CHAPTER 1

The Prisoner

Rook knew that things were not going according to plan.

He jumped from boam to beam, pulling his companion along with him, the prisoner he'd just released. "Hurry!" he whisper-shouted, although he knew no amount of coaxing would help. The prisoner's legs were encased in metal, the joints stiff from disuse. His arms were still flesh, however, which made it somewhat easier to keep a grip on him.

"I can't," the prisoner panted. "I . . . need . . . to . . . stop. . . ."

Rook paused to let him rest, balanced precariously on a narrow girder that hung across a stretch of empty space. Below them lay a black abyss. Above them a maze of steel girders wound upward in a twisted skeleton, blocking out most of the churning, red sky.

It sickened him to be back in the Fortress of Chaós again, the dark castle at the edge of Skot'os, the lair of Ponéros, the enemy. Rook had escaped from this place not long before, rescued by a group of schoolkids who had brought him a message: *Once freed, always free*. He'd returned to bring that message to another prisoner. He'd also brought a key. It was the same key that had been taken back from the enemy by the kids—the key that opened prison doors. He reached into his pocket, fingering the long shining object with the scroll-y handle, making sure it was still there. He couldn't lose it, whatever happened.

"This way." He beckoned to his companion to follow him along the beam. The boots that Ruwach had given Rook gripped the steel girder like rubber, giving him assurance he wouldn't slip. But the prisoner's metal feet scraped eerily, making Rook's hair stand on end. He remembered all too well what it felt like to hobble along on metal feet. And how he had been restored, thanks to those kids. And to Ruwach, the one who had sent them.

If only Rook had thought this through a little more. Getting into the fortress had been easy, *too* easy. The narrow beam of light from his breastplate had lit up his path with each step. No one tried to stop him. The Forgers—the fully mechanized soldiers of Ponéros's evil army—were nowhere in sight. Yet Rook had had the feeling he was being watched. The Ents, perhaps, those nasty metal bugs that liked to pass themselves off as butterflies. They'd probably been tracking him with their red laser eyes, unseen.

Rook should have known better than to simply go out the same way he'd gone in. But he was so determined to free a soul and get out of that horrible place as soon as he could, he hadn't taken proper precautions. He thought he knew the way. But the fortress seemed to have shifted around him, morphed—his path wiped away, every exit he had known blocked.

Chaos. Confusion. *That* was Ponéros's security system.

The beam under them shuddered, forcing them to stop. Loud booms filled the air around them, the sound of heavy footsteps echoing through the maze of girders.

"It's them," said the prisoner in a squeaky, pathetic voice. "They're coming now."

Forgers, Rook thought. They had trapped him. Now they would come to retake him and the prisoner both.

"What's your name?" Rook asked.

"It's . . . F-f-finn," stuttered the prisoner

"Well, Finn, we have to get to the end of this beam. And then . . . we'll figure something out." He hoped his voice didn't sound as hopeless as he felt. He inched his way along the slender path, keeping one hand on Finn's arm so he wouldn't lose his balance and tumble into the abyss underneath them.

After what seemed like forever, he got to the end of the girder and grabbed a vertical beam that projected from the empty space below. Finn grabbed on as well. The whole structure trembled and shook with the sound of approaching Forgers. Red, round, glowing orbs appeared in the inky blackness, closing in around them.

"Which way?" whispered Finn.

Rook looked up. He couldn't really see anything but small angular blotches of red sky peeking through the tangled web of beams overhead.

"Up here!"

The voice seemed to come from the sky. A young voice. A *girl's* voice.

Rook strained to see who had spoken. Stars seemed to be pouring in from the cracks in the girders above them. Not stars . . . *Sparks* . . . those tiny, brilliant balls of light that dwelled in the Cave. *Ruwach had come!* But the voice was not Ruwach's. . . . It definitely belonged to a young girl.

"Come *on*, will you?" the girl's voice scolded him. By the light of the Sparks he could just see the outline of a human standing on a girder above him.

"This way! Climb!"

How in the world did that human—a girl—get all the way up there? Maybe it was a trick. Ponéros was good at tricks. Deception was his game. Yet what choice did Rook have but to follow?

He turned to Finn, whose half-human face stared back at him, fear roiling in his eyes. "Did you see that?" he asked, pointing upward.

A huge Forger vaulted onto the girder they'd just crossed, its metal fists closed and ready to strike. As the Forger lunged for him, Rook drew his sword and swung, slicing off one of its metal arms. The Forger bellowed, its red eyes spinning with rage. It stumbled backward and fell from the beam to the dark void below. But soon there was another one to take its place. And another.

"Great," Rook muttered to himself.

"You coming or what?" said the voice above him.

"How am I supposed to . . . ?"

"Use your belt!"

The belt!

Rook suddenly understood. As the second Forger charged him, Rook took off his belt—a wide, plain white belt that had no visible clasp. He tossed one end upward. It stretched out to several times its own length, the end wrapping snugly around a beam above. The belt, stretched thin, began to hum like a tightly wound guitar string. "Hold on to me!" Rook said and jumped, his boots launching him and the prisoner into the air as more Forgers converged under them. Rook swung one leg over the beam on which his belt was wrapped, hauling himself and Finn over the top.

"Piece of cake," he said breathlessly, giving Finn a little encouraging smile. Finn tried to smile back with his half-metal face.

"You're too slow!" said the girl, who had scrambled up to an even higher perch.

That girl was starting to get on Rook's nerves.

Rook looked down, saw the Forgers climbing up the steel girders toward him. *Pretty nimble,* he thought, *for big, hulking hardware.* He unwrapped his belt, threw one end up to yet another beam and jumped again, holding tightly onto Finn.

Rook could see the girl more clearly now. She had scrambled up toward the top of the fortress, where bare beams thrust into the swirling, red-purple sky. Her fiery red hair whipped around her face in the biting wind. She held on with one hand, glancing out over the expanse of sky.

"Come *on*, already!"

Rook jumped again, Finn clinging to him, the belt propelling them ever upward. Below them Forgers continued to gather, scaling the beams, their red eyes piercing the darkness. Where on earth was that girl going? She seemed to be leading him into a trap.

When finally Rook and his half-human charge made it to the pinnacle, the little girl with red hair greeted them with a big sigh.

"Took you long enough," she snipped.

"Hey, you try dragging up a two-hundred-pound hunk of metal—no offense." Rook glanced at Finn in apology then turned back to the girl. He unwrapped his belt and refastened it around his waist, making sure his sword was still secure. The girl, he noticed, didn't have a sword, only a belt, breastplate, and boots. Like those other kids, he remembered. The ones who had rescued him. But this girl hadn't been with them when they'd come for him. Again, he wondered if this was a trap—if this girl was working for Ponéros himself.

"Who are you, by the way? Did Ruwach send you? How are we getting out of here?"

"We're going to jump, of course!"

"What?" Rook blinked, hoping he'd heard her wrong. The beam on which they were perched shook with the vibrations of the Forgers clambering toward them.

"Now!" the girl said, with something like glee. "Let's go!"

Before he had time to react, she'd grabbed his arm and jumped straight into the turbulent sky, taking Rook and Finn with her.

CHAPTER 2

Rain

Evan sat on the school bus, staring at the rain-drops cascading down the window. He liked how they would run straight down and then suddenly turn toward each other, joining together to make a bigger raindrop that raced down the glass even faster. It made Evan wonder why they did that—fuse and then fall. Interesting. Did raindrops just want to be together? Was it more fun that way?

The bus was filling up, kids laughing and joking, relaxing after a long day of school. The older kids went straight to the back, the little kids sitting up front. Evan sat in the middle of the bus. He kept his eyes on the window, watching the raindrops. It was better than seeing the faces of the other kids as they looked him over and then passed by.

He was a month into fourth grade at his new school, and still he hadn't made a real friend. The kids at Cedar Creek Elementary had their own friend groups. They weren't looking for any new members. Kids here were different from the city, where he used to go to school. Most of them had grown up in the same place and known each other forever. New kids didn't come to their school too often.

Give it time, his dad had said. Evan wondered how long "time" would take.

He heard giggling and looked across the aisle. Two girls glanced at him, smirking and whispering. Probably laughing at him because of his hair. His mom had put some stuff in it to get it to lay down flat for Picture Day. Picture Day. The worst day of the school year. He had to wear a collared shirt that itched his neck, and his mom made him promise to not get it dirty all day. Thank goodness that was over.

He counted on his fingers—eight months to go before summer came back. It seemed like an eternity.

A little kid sat down next to him, a second-grader probably. With a runny nose. Like most second-graders. He wiped his nose with his hand and then wiped his hand on the back of the seat. Evan looked away. Disgusting. The kid started bouncing in his seat, like he couldn't wait for the bus to get going. Annoying. Little kids could never just sit still.

"What's your name?" the kid asked him.

"Evan." Evan made a point of not asking the kid his name, just so the kid would know that Evan didn't really care. He might be desperate for friends, but not for bouncy, runny-nosed second-grader friends.

"I'm Charlie," said the kid. "Where do you live?"

"Around," Evan answered. Maybe the kid would get a clue that he didn't really want to talk.

Finally, the bus lurched into motion and Charlie stopped bouncing, his attention elsewhere. Evan settled back in his seat. It was a twenty-minute ride to his house. Maybe now he could have a little peace and quiet.

He pulled his phone out of his backpack and turned it on. It was his day to have the phone, which he shared with his older brother, Xavier, although Xavier seemed to get it a lot more than he did.

He opened his favorite game, *Kingdom Quest*. Evan loved this game. He was even better than his brother at it, although he was now stuck on level six. The player had to use blocks of all different shapes and sizes to build a castle before it was attacked by the Icemen, who were like an army of creatures made of ice and snow who would come and destroy the castle if it wasn't finished in time. In each level of play, the castle you had to build got more complicated. In order to get building blocks, you had to go through a series of challenges, like defeating a tribe of trolls or decoding a secret scroll. Evan loved stuff like that. He wasn't allowed to use the phone in school, but he figured the bus didn't count as actual school anyway.

Evan played intently for several minutes, but still he failed to finish before the Icemen came and destroyed his castle. He sighed, tapping the reset button. At least he got to start over and try again. Eventually, he knew he would win. He would go on to the next level and a brand-new set of challenges to overcome.

The game sort of reminded him of Ahoratos—the real but unseen world he had been to twice with Xavier and his other friends. Each time they went, the challenge was a little tougher, but if they followed the instruction from The Book and listened to their guide Ruwach, they would make it through. Best of all, even if they messed up, they got a second chance. At least, so far.

He thought about his friends, Levi, Brianna, and Manuel, his fellow Prince Warriors. He wished he could go to school with them—they were at Cedar Creek Middle. They could all hang out, have lunch together, talk about their adventures in Ahoratos without being looked at like they were weird. When Evan had boasted to the other kids in his class how he'd gone over a waterfall and battled evil butterflies and ridden a flying dragon, they just looked at him like he was crazy. Making it all up.

Maybe he was. It was more than a month since he'd been to Ahoratos. Maybe it had been just a dream. Except Xavier had been there too—could two people dream the same dream at the same time? Evan doubted it.

Yet ever since they'd rescued the prisoner Rook and escaped from that evil Fortress of Chaós in Skot'os, none of them had heard a word from Ruwach. Maybe he was on vacation, or taking an extra long nap. Or maybe he just didn't need the Prince Warriors anymore.

Maybe it was all in Evan's imagination.

Maybe they were never going back.

But they *had* to go back. For one thing, they didn't have their full sets of armor. Only the belt, breastplate, and boots. A real Warrior needed more than that. They still had to get the shield, the helmet, and the sword. The sword—that's what Evan really wanted. A real, beautiful, majestic sword. A Forger-slaying sword.

If he had that sword, those two girls in the next seat would be too busy staring in awe to even think of making fun of him.

The bus stopped at the Rec. That's what he and the others called the Cedar Creek Recreational Center. Most of the kids, including Charlie with the runny nose, got off the bus. Normally Evan would have gotten off there too. Xavier and his friends were probably there already, playing basketball. But Evan didn't want to play basketball in his itchy, button-down shirt, and he'd forgotten to bring an extra set of clothes. He would just go home to change and ask his mom to drive him over to the Rec later.

When the bus screeched to a stop at his house, Evan got up, shoving his phone in his backpack. He walked quickly toward the front as the folding doors squealed open to let him out. The rain had let up a bit, but he put up his hood anyway. It was a long walk to his house; the pebble driveway dipped down toward a bridge over the creek and up another hill. Evan liked to imagine he was back in Ahoratos again, running through the woods, jumping over the deep chasm that separated Skot'os, the dark side of Ahoratos, from the rest of that golden kingdom. He liked to imagine he was building the bridge with his feet, as he had done the last time he was there. That had been amazing—stepping up into the sky, the stones forming under his boots as he went . . .

"You gonna just stand there admiring the view?"

Evan turned to the voice—Miss Lois, the bus driver. Her crinkly eyes smiled at him. She had spiky gray hair and lots of red lipstick; she reminded Evan of a kindly, grandmotherly sort of gargoyle.

"Sorry," he muttered, jumping off the bus.

"You take care now, Evan," Miss Lois said, shutting the doors. The bus rumbled away.

Evan watched it go, bouncing over ruts in the road, fountains of muddy water shooting up from the wheels.

The wheels of the bus go round and round. . . .

What made him think of that baby song? That snot-nosed kid Charlie, probably. *You need to get a grip,* he said to himself. *You're a Prince Warrior, right? Not a little kid anymore.*

It was still raining, so he put up his hood and was about to head down the drive when he remembered: the mail. Because it was such a long walk from the road to the house, his mom had told him and his brother to please stop and check the mailbox whenever they were on their way home. Xavier usually forgot, but Evan didn't mind getting the mail. It was like having a job, in a way. And it always gave him brownie points with

Mom, who liked it when he remembered to do things without being told a hundred times.

He walked over to the mailbox, which was nestled in a bunch of tall brownish stalks his mother called "grass." It didn't look like grass to Evan, but Mom had lots of weird names for things. He pulled on the mailbox door. It stuck, as it always did, so he had to pull extra hard. The box was full. Mondays—it was always the fullest on Mondays.

He pulled out the letters and magazines, balancing them so he wouldn't drop any on the wet ground.

He'd just gotten everything out and folded the magazines around the letters securely when he heard something—a zap, a sizzle, like an electric spark. He thought at first an overhead wire had been hit by lightning, although he hadn't seen any lightning. This wasn't a lightning kind of rain.

He looked up at the tall poles that held the wires like tightropes all the way down the road. Out of the corner of his eye he saw a flash. But it didn't come from the pole. It came from the house across the street.

He squinted at the house. Manuel lived there. He'd been amazed to discover that Manuel lived right across the street from him. Evan hadn't actually been to Manuel's house, mainly because Manuel had never invited him. Manuel kept to himself most of the time, probably studying the effects of photon rays on ladybugs or building an anti-gravity machine in his room.

Another flash. Maybe Manuel was messing with something even worse than anti-gravity. (Evan wasn't exactly sure what anti-gravity was, but it sounded kind of dangerous.) He stood still for a moment, unsure of what to do. But then there was another flash that lasted even longer, and Evan felt sure something was really wrong. Maybe there was a . . . *fire*! He sprinted into action, holding the mail under one arm like a football as he ran across the street and up the steep driveway to Manuel's house.

He didn't notice that one of the letters in his bundle, a bright red envelope, had slipped out and tumbled into the tall brownish stalks beside the mailbox. As it fell, it let off a sprinkle of light. But Evan didn't notice that either.

CHAPTER 3

A Narrow Escape

We're going to die now.

That and other dismal thoughts filled Rook's mind as he and Finn and the girl with the red hair plummeted toward the rocky landscape below. Dense fog swirled around blackened trees. Scraggy mountain peaks stood like giant spikes, ready to impale them.

Rook closed his eyes. He didn't want to see what he was about to crash into.

Suddenly he hit something, and he felt his stomach lurch up into his throat. But the something on which he landed kept moving, as if he were still falling.

Rook felt the wind rush into his eyes as he opened them, gazing into the turbulent red sky. He had landed—all three of them had landed—on something slimy and scaly, and they were wedged between wide spikes. . . .

Tannyn!

Rook laughed out loud as he realized they were sitting on the back of a familiar friend, the flying dragon/sea monster with wings as wide as a 747. The red-haired girl was laughing too.

"You could have told me!" Rook shouted over the roar of the wind. Tannyn swerved to avoid a skypod, one of many huge, lumpy gray objects that floated in the angry sky.

"That wouldn't have been any fun!" the girl shouted back, her voice nearly carried off in the wind. "I'm Ivy, by the way!"

"Oh—I'm Rook! This is—Finn—" Rook nodded toward the half-metal prisoner who clung to one of Tannyn's spikes. Finn looked way too petrified to answer.

"Yeah, I know. Ruwach told me. Hang on!"

The dragon dipped into valleys and careened around mountains. Rook knew Tannyn was just having fun more than anything. He didn't get out of the water very often.

Rook glanced down and saw a gray cloud racing toward them. "Ents! Below!" he shouted to Tannyn, who drew back his head and let out a stream of blue fire. The large metallic insects, like mechanized butterflies, shrieked in alarm, the sound like a thousand nails against a thousand chalkboards. The humans winced at the awful sound, unable to cover their ears because they had to hold on tight to Tannyn's spikes. But the blast of fire-breath gave Tannyn a clear path through the swarm.

"Good boy!" Rook shouted once they were out of danger. The Ent swarm tried to follow but couldn't keep up with Tannyn, who, once he got going, was as fast as a golden eagle diving for prey.

The sky changed from red to gold as they passed over the chasm that separated Skot'os from the other side of Ahoratos. The Bridge of Tears—the only bridge that spanned the chasm—changed from a network of black metal girders to quaint, moss-covered cobblestones. The landscape changed as well: the mountains looked majestic rather than threatening, the forests went from black and forbidding to green and rolling. Flowers appeared, breaking up the rolling green meadows with wild splashes of color. They were far enough away from the fortress now; Rook began to relax and enjoy the ride.

"What . . . is . . . this thing?" The former prisoner shouted to Rook as if he'd just recovered himself enough to speak. "It looks like a—*dragon*—"

"Oh, yeah," Rook yelled back at him. "Tannyn is sort of a dragon, but not exactly. He's not dangerous. At least, not to us."

"He's good for roasting marshmallows too!" Ivy added with a laugh.

They circled around a wide, very tall mountain, so tall it disappeared into a cloud above. It was the tallest mountain by far in the kingdom of Ahoratos. Rook glanced back to see Finn's awed expression.

"What . . . is . . . this mountain?" gasped the prisoner, unable to take in the size of it.

"You'll find out, eventually," Rook said.

Suddenly, Tannyn swerved and dove straight for a shorter peak ringed by white, puffy clouds.

"Hey! We're going to crash!" shouted Finn, who saw the mountain coming straight for them. The other two only laughed.

"Better hang on!" Rook yelled. "Tannyn's not great on landings."

Tannyn barreled into the clouds, which parted to reveal a huge, shining castle. Finn gasped at the endless array of turrets and towers, almost forgetting to hang on as the dragon bumped and slid across the wide courtyard, skidding to a halt in front of a large, ornate gate that gleamed as if it were made of diamonds.

"He's better at water landings," Ivy said. Rook laughed. Finn looked stunned, his human parts turning green like he was going to be sick.

Tannyn opened his mouth as if preparing to let out another stream of fire. "Gorp." It sounded like a prolonged burp. The huge creature folded his wings and lowered his head so his passengers could dismount. Ivy went first, scrambling down Tannyn's long neck to the smooth marble pavement. Rook followed, helping Finn negotiate the dragon's spiky neck to get to solid ground.

"You okay?" Rook asked the former prisoner. Finn nodded, still wobbly. He gazed in awe at the beautiful castle in front of him. A castle nestled in the clouds, sparkling brilliantly in the sun. He shook his head in disbelief.

"Yes . . . I'm okay, but . . . am I really . . . free?" he stuttered.

"Yes, thanks to Ruwach," Rook said.

"Who?"

Just then the shining gate began to open, revealing a very tiny creature cloaked in purple. His face was hidden deep inside the purple hood, although Rook thought he could see two small radiant lights that might have been eyes peering out at them.

"Ruwach!" said Ivy happily, running to him. She reached down to give Ruwach a hug around his cloaked neck. Rook had never seen anyone touch—let alone hug—Ruwach before.

"Good to see you, Princess Ivy," Ruwach said in his large, sonorous voice, so much bigger than his tiny form. He turned to Rook, who knelt, bowing his head, one hand on the hilt of his sword. "And you, Prince Rook. You released another prisoner; well done. I'm glad to see you managed to find your way back."

Rook could hear the slight sarcasm in Ruwach's tone. "I was fine," he said, with a sidelong glance at Ivy. "But . . . I appreciate the extra help."

"No biggie," said Ivy, smirking at him.

"Anyway, this is . . ."

"Finn," said Ruwach, the hood turning toward Finn. "You have been a prisoner a long time, haven't you?"

Finn nodded, glancing down at his mostly metal body. This was what happened to prisoners in Skot'os. They gradually turned to metal, their humanness fading away, until they looked no different from the Forgers—the fearsome minions of Ponéros, the enemy. "There isn't much left of me to save."

"Do you want to be healed?"

Finn looked down at the little guide, surprised. "You—can do that?"

"I can. But you must want it."

Finn tried to nod a sure affirmation, although his head would not move much.

"Of course I do. I mean, who wouldn't?"

"You would be surprised," said Ruwach with a deep sigh. The little guide approached Finn slowly, raising one of his long, draped arms. A hand emerged from the cloak, each finger a thin white flame. Finn drew back nervously, but the hand reached for him, touching his metal skin. The touch was very warm, burning through the metal parts of him. He gasped but soon felt the hard shell begin to melt off of him, turning to a fine dust that floated away on the breeze. He suddenly felt lighter, freer than he had ever felt before. He looked at his legs, both of them turned to human flesh. He touched his face—it was no longer cold and hard, but soft, like real skin. He fell to his knees, bowing before Ruwach, weeping with relief and gratitude.

Rook watched this scene, his heart twisting with the memory of his own melting, not so long ago. Having received that gift for himself, he was determined to help free as many prisoners as possible. It was why he returned to Skot'os over and over again, despite the danger.

Once freed, always free.

Those were the words that had melted his chains.

"You have the key, Prince Rook?" Ruwach asked.

Rook nodded, pulling the long, shiny black key from his pocket and holding it like a delicate, invaluable gem. This was the key that had opened his own prison cell not that long ago. It had an ornate, scroll-y bow with an odd-shaped bit that extended from the tip.

"I will keep this safe until you return." Ruwach turned to Ivy. "Princess Ivy, I believe you already know what I need you to do now," he said softly.

For the first time, Ivy looked uncertain. "I'm not really sure I'm the right person for the job."

"You are the right one," Ruwach said, patting her shoulder. "Do not be afraid, Princess Ivy. You know that when I give you a task, I also give you everything you need to complete it."

Ivy smiled, nodding. She gave Ruwach another quick hug then stepped back, standing beside Rook as the gate and the castle began to fade, engulfed in clouds. From somewhere in his fading vision, Rook heard Ruwach's voice, distant and yet very close, as if coming from inside his own mind:

Keep a close eye on the children. . . .

CHAPTER 4

The Useless Seed

Evan knocked frantically on the door of Manuel's house and rang the doorbell several times. After a few minutes, the door finally opened. A man with a short crew cut glowered at him over half-rimmed glasses, a book in his hand. Evan took a small step backward.

He'd never actually met Manuel's father before, although he had seen him picking Manuel up at the rec center a few times. Mr. Santos was always really stern and silent; he never talked to anyone. Manuel had said his dad was a college professor, and so Evan figured he was probably really smart and didn't have much time for people who weren't as smart as he was. Or maybe it was because Manuel's mom had died the year before, and his dad was still really sad about that.

"Can I help you?" asked Manuel's dad in a clipped, Spanish accent. Something in his dark gaze made Evan quake a little, as if he had picked the absolute worst time to visit.

"Um . . . Hello. Mr. Santos? I'm Evan . . . from over there—" Evan indicated the property across the street. "I'm a friend of Manuel's. I was getting off the bus, and I saw something . . . in the window up there . . . thought there might be trouble . . ."

"Trouble?" The man sighed, his expression softening a bit. "There is no trouble. I can assure you. That's just Manuel. Doing an experiment. Happens all the time. . . . What did you say your name was?"

"Evan."

"Oh, yes. Evan. Manuel mentioned you, I believe. Come in, if you want." He called up the stairs. "Manuel! Evan está aquí!"

Evan glanced around quickly as he moved toward the staircase. He noticed a room to his left; the door was ajar, and he could see that it was jammed with books and papers. Probably Mr. Santos's study. The shelves contained what looked like lots and lots of rocks and artifacts and stuff that smart people collect.

He was just about to look away when something caught his eye. There, centered on the stately wooden desk was . . . a book. A large book with pages that seemed worn and aged. Something about it—the size, the frayed edges, the sketched image he could see faintly on the opened page—all of it seemed familiar to Evan. He squinted curiously and leaned closer toward the door to get a better look, but Mr. Santos blocked his way, half closing the door.

"Go on up. First door on the left. Excuse me. I have some work to do." Manuel's dad slipped through the door, shutting it behind him. Evan shrugged to himself and darted quickly up the steps. He went down the hallway, past a door on his right—a neat bedroom with hardly anything in it. Manuel wasn't in there. Evan kept going until he reached the door on the left. It was slightly open, so he peeked in through the opening then knocked lightly. There was no response. He could see Manuel hunched over something, working intently, but Evan couldn't tell what he was doing. Evan carefully pushed the door open and gazed around the room. He had never seen anything like it.

Manuel's room looked more like a mad scientist's laboratory than a bedroom. Books and mason jars containing bizarre specimens lined the shelves along the wall. In the window sat several weird-looking plants in pots. Manuel's desk was covered in more mason jars and beakers, books and papers, and a computer. A mobile of the solar system hung over the bed, on which lay a rumpled bedspread imprinted with a huge picture of Albert Einstein, his spiky wisps of white hair shooting all the way up to the pillow. There wasn't a single bit of shelf space or desk space or even floor space left bare.

Manuel was bent over a tiny object hooked up to electrodes. He appeared to be waiting for it to do something. He was so intent on his mission that he didn't even hear Evan knock on the door for the second time.

"Manuel?" Evan said.

Manuel lurched upright, his thick red glasses nearly flying off his face.

"Evan?" he said, shocked. "What are you . . . ? How did you get here?"

"I live across the street, remember?"

"Oh, right . . . of course . . ." Manuel shook his head as if clearing out cobwebs. "I forgot."

"I saw something flashing from your window. I thought there was a fire. . . ."

"Flashes? Fire?" Manuel looked perplexed. "No, there hasn't been anything like that. At least not today anyway. You must be mistaken." He returned to staring at the tiny object as if he'd forgotten about Evan already.

"I definitely saw a flash," Evan said, although he secretly wondered if he had possibly just imagined it. "Why are you electrocuting . . . a Skittle?" He pointed to the object that was hooked up to the electrodes. It did look exactly like a Skittle.

"Skittle?" Manuel said. Then he shook his head. "No, no. This is a seed."

"Why are you electrocuting a seed?"

"I'm not *electrocuting* anything. I'm just testing it, to see if there is any electrical activity."

"In a seed?"

"Yes. Well, it's not an ordinary seed. At least, I don't think it is. That's what I'm trying to find out. But it's really no use. It's not doing a thing."

Manuel pulled the electrodes off the seed and picked it up. He held it in his open hand so Evan could see it better. Still looked like a Skittle. A red one.

"Never saw a seed like that," Evan said. "Where did you get it?"

"It belonged to my mother. She kept it in this little jewelry box on her dresser. I used to ask her about it—she said it was special. Powerful."

"What kind of powerful?"

"She never explained that part." Manuel put the seed under the microscope and began turning the knobs.

"Your mom didn't tell you where she got it?"

"Nope. She said she would someday—but she never got a chance, I guess." Manuel kept his eyes down, but Evan could feel his uneasiness at the topic of his mother.

"Oh, yeah. My mom does that to me too," Evan said with a little laugh, trying to lighten the mood. "I mean, she tells me she'll explain something someday, but then she never does."

The two boys smiled at each other. Evan had always thought Manuel was a little weird. For starters, he was more like a grown-up than a kid. He had glasses and really short hair, just like his dad. He even dressed like his dad, in khakis with sharp creases and collared shirts. And he always had his nose in a book or a science experiment. When he talked he used big words that made the whole conversation turn to mush in Evan's mind.

But after their last adventure, Evan had started to appreciate Manuel's good qualities. He was super smart, for one thing. And Manuel had even proved, when he'd retrieved the prison key from the Forger, that he could be a little brave too.

"Your room is . . . pretty wild," Evan said, looking around. He saw a large round rock on a shelf and picked it up. To his surprise, it fell open in his hands, split right down the middle. The inside was purple and swirl-y with a hollow center. "Um . . . I think I broke this." He showed the two halves to Manuel.

Manuel glanced up to see what Evan was looking at. "No, you didn't. It's a geode," Manuel said. "My dad cut it open to show me the crystals on the inside."

"Cool. So how did the crystals get inside the rock?"

"It's hard to explain. . . . Imagine a hollow in the ground, like a rabbit hole. Water seeps into the hole. Water is full of minerals. It dries up, but the minerals build up and become crystallized."

"Sweet. Where'd you get it?"

"My dad and I went on a geode hunt once—in Arizona. My dad likes rocks. He's a geologist."

"What's that?"

"Someone who studies rocks."

"I thought he was a college professor."

"He is. He teaches geology."

"That's cool," said Evan. "Do you and your dad go on a lot of trips like that?"

"Not anymore. We used to, when my mom was . . ." Manuel's voice dropped off. Then he said in a quieter tone: "Anyway, now he spends most of his time in his den, when he's not at the college."

"Oh . . . so was your mom a geometrist too?"

"*Geologist*. And no, she was a botanist."

"A what?"

"She studied plants."

"Oh."

"I assumed this seed was some rare specimen. It looks similar to a species from South America, which is where she came from. But when she said it was powerful . . ." Manuel's voice trailed off. Evan could tell he didn't really want to talk anymore about his mom.

Evan poked around some more. Below the shelf was a crate containing many round, smooth black stones. He tried to pick one up, but it stuck. He had to yank to get it free. "Whoa. Are these magnets?"

"What? Oh, yes. Lodestones, actually. Naturally magnetic rocks."

"You collect those too?"

"Birthday present," Manuel mumbled.

"So you get mostly rocks for your birthday? Sweet." Evan played with the lodestones for a while, using one to pick up a bunch more to see how many he could string together. When he got bored he wandered over to the window and inspected the goofy-looking plants. One of them looked almost alien, with large red spiky leaves like claws. He reached out to touch it.

"Don't do that!" Manuel said. "It bites."

"The plant . . . bites?"

"It's a Venus flytrap."

"Really? It's from Venus?"

"No, not actually Venus. It does trap flies, however. And occasionally fingers."

"Can I see?"

Manuel reached over and touched the leaf with a pencil. The leaf closed quickly, like a jaw clamping shut.

"Cool!" said Evan. "Maybe I'll get one of these for Xavier for Christmas. I just won't tell him what it does." He giggled. "Until it's too late."

Manuel didn't respond. He was still peering intently in the microscope. Evan watched him a moment.

"Have you tried planting it?" Evan asked after a few seconds of silence. He was getting a tad bored. "Like in the ground?"

"Yes, of course. I put it in a hydroponic solution." He looked up, saw Evan's blank expression, and knew that he needed to explain. "That's a nutrient solution for growing seeds without soil. But it didn't do anything. I tried boiling it too."

"Boiling it? What for?"

"Some seeds need to be boiled or scratched or digested before they will germinate."

"Digested? You mean like *eaten*?" Evan made a face of disgust. "Gross. Maybe you should feed it to the flytrap."

"I tried. The flytrap wouldn't take it. It prefers meat."

"Meat?" Evan said, paling slightly.

"Hamburger."

Evan sat down on the bed and looked up at the mobile. The planets had stopped rotating around the sun. He reached up and gave them a little shove to get them going again. He wondered where Ahoratos fit in among the planets, or if it was even meant to fit in at all.

"You heard anything?" he asked. "From . . . you know who?"

"Who?" Manuel looked up, perplexed for a few long moments. "Oh. No. Not a thing."

"Did you get a message today?"

"Uh . . . no. Actually."

"That's kind of weird, isn't it? There should have been a message. An instruction." Yesterday's message had been mysterious. It had popped up on the screen of his cell phone while he was eating a bowl of cereal for an afternoon snack:

Ask and it shall be given.

Evan wasn't sure what that meant. The instructions were usually a bit confusing at first, but then something would happen, and it would all make sense. He'd learned to be patient about stuff like that.

Evan scratched his ear and gave the mobile another shove.

Suddenly another flash filled the room. The lights went out, and Manuel's computer shut down. Manuel looked up, annoyed.

"What did you do? Did you hit a switch or something?" he asked Evan.

"I didn't touch anything except the mobile," Evan said, holding up his hands. "Honest."

"Well, this is strange. Maybe a power line went down. Very annoying. I guess this experiment will have to wait until later."

Evan smiled at this. He was ready to do something else. "Hey, want to play a game?"

"A game?" Manuel looked at Evan as if he didn't know what he was talking about.

"Yeah, don't you have any board games? Like Sorry or Monopoly?" Evan started rummaging through Manuel's shelves in search of a game.

"Please don't touch my things. . . ." Manuel protested.

"Hey!" Evan exclaimed, pulling a large and dusty book from the shelf. He held the familiar volume and ran his hand quickly over the raised image of the Crest of Ahoratos on the cover. He looked at Manuel. "This is the same book I have. I forgot you had one too. Didn't your mom give you this?"

"Yes. . . . Can you just put it back?" Manuel reached for the book, but Evan snatched it away in time, laughing. "Be careful with that!" Manuel said. "It's very delicate. . . ."

"Hey look. . . ." Evan held the book up, staring intently at the cover. "Your cover glows in the dark. Mine doesn't do that."

"It does not glow in the dark—"

"Yes it does. See?" Evan turned the book so Manuel could see the cover. The funny-shaped ℵ, the Crest of Ahoratos, was indeed glowing red.

"It's never done that before," Manuel said. As they both stared, the symbol grew brighter until it actually lifted off the book itself and hovered in the air before them, turning slowly.

"Are you seeing what I'm seeing?" Manuel asked, blinking to make sure it was really there.

"Yeah, I'm seeing it."

"It can't be real, can it?" Manuel reached out to touch the floating Crest.

"Wait!" said Evan. "We should do this together. That way, if something happens, it'll happen to both of us."

Manuel swallowed. "Okay. Ready?"

Evan nodded. Together they reached toward the shimmering Crest. As soon as their fingers touched it, a gigantic flash filled their vision. A stark whiteness like a blinding light had just been turned on over their heads.

Evan shut his eyes, waiting for it to pass. But when he opened them again, the whiteness was still there. He looked at Manuel in confusion. Manuel's room was gone. The whole world seemed to have disappeared.

CHAPTER 5

A New Friend

Brianna unlocked her phone and opened the app called "UNSEEN." Still nothing. No message, no instruction. Every day there had been a message on her screen, but today it was just the weird symbols and patterns that didn't make any sense. Again.

She pushed the lock button on her phone and turned her attention to the boys' basketball game, which was taking place in the gym due to the bad weather. Levi and Xavier were both playing, as was Landon. That was something to see. Landon, the big bully whom she and Levi had confronted only a month before, was now playing ball *with* Levi and the other kids. And Landon was pretty good too. Wonders never cease. Brianna knew Levi didn't really like shooting hoops very much;

he wouldn't be playing basketball at all if it hadn't been raining. He'd be out at the skateboard park with his buddies.

Xavier made a basket, and a group of girls in the stands cheered. Xavier lived and breathed basketball. He was tall and sinewy, with long legs that seemed to be able to cover the whole court in a few strides. Levi was shorter and stockier, not as quick in basketball, but on a skateboard he could dip and turn like an acrobat.

Levi recovered the ball and started dribbling down the court. Mr. J. Ar, Levi's dad who volunteered most days at the rec center, trotted up and down the court with his whistle in his mouth, blowing it occasionally. Mr. J. Ar (short for James Arthur) loved basketball almost as much as Xavier. Evan did too. . . . Where was Evan anyway? She looked around but didn't see him.

"Is someone sitting here?" asked a soft, tentative voice. Brianna looked up at the girl with glossy red hair and soft freckles. She was pointing to the space next to Brianna on the bench.

"Uh, guess not," Brianna mumbled, picking up her phone as if she had just gotten an important text.

"I'm . . . Ivy," said the girl.

"Yeah, I know."

Ivy sat down, turning her eyes to the game. Brianna noticed how Ivy's hair fell in tumbling waves down her back, how her jeans looked new and she had on one of those hip new sling backpacks with the bright pattern, just like the cool, seventh-grade girls seemed to have. Brianna quickly shoved her own backpack under her seat. She'd had it since elementary school, and it had been her sister's before that. Brianna had three older sisters, so she never got anything new.

Brianna remembered the day that Ivy had joined her and Levi in standing up to Landon when he was bullying Manuel. Since then, they had spoken a few times. Brianna had a feeling that Ivy wanted to be friends. But Brianna wasn't sure she wanted Ivy for a friend. For one thing, Ivy's hair was a little too perfect. For another thing, Brianna was a Princess Warrior, and she knew Ivy would never understand what that meant.

"I like your headband," Ivy said, startling her. Brianna looked at her and gave a small smile.

"Oh, thanks."

"Where'd you get it?"

"Nowhere. . . . I made it."

Brianna wished she hadn't said that. She should have mentioned some expensive boutique or department store. Now Ivy would think she was a big loser.

"It's . . . really pretty," Ivy murmured.

"Thanks." Brianna glanced at Ivy and saw her fiddling with a lock of her hair, twirling it around and around one finger. Her face was all red, like she was really nervous or embarrassed about something. When Ivy looked her way, Brianna turned her attention back to her phone.

"Um . . . I was wondering . . ." Ivy began.

"What?" Brianna said.

Finally, Ivy just sighed. "Oh . . . nothing."

Brianna wished the girl would just go away, or at least not talk anymore. She didn't want to answer a lot of questions about where she lived or why she lived with her grandparents instead of her real parents. Ivy probably lived in a big house and had her own room. Just like most of the other girls in her class.

Brianna pulled a tube of her favorite glitter lip gloss out of her hoodie pocket and slathered it on her lips. She always felt a lot prettier with sparkly lips. But then all of the sudden she felt stupid again—Ivy didn't wear glitter lip gloss. None of the girls in sixth grade wore it. She should have grown out of it long ago. She tucked the tube back in her pocket, rubbing her lips together and wiping them with the back of her hand.

The whistle blew, and Brianna breathed out a sigh of relief, glad to get away from this annoyingly pretty girl. She raced down the bleachers to greet Levi and Xavier.

"Good game!" she said. Levi was sweating like crazy and still panting from the game. He nodded to her. Ivy walked passed them both, smiling a little shyly but not saying anything.

"It was all right," Levi said.

Xavier knocked him on the shoulder. "Better luck next time."

"Yeah, you better watch out," Levi answered.

Landon walked up to Levi. They bumped fists wordlessly before Landon went on his way.

"You guys like BFFs now?" Brianna asked with a short giggle.

"He's okay," said Levi with a shrug. "I mean, he's not bullying the little kids anymore. That's something."

They walked to the main room of the rec center, where kids were gathering their books and coats, preparing to go home. Outside it was getting dark, the rain still pounding the roof and streaming down the windows. Xavier stooped to get a drink from the water fountain.

"Where's Evan?" Brianna asked him.

"Guess he didn't come today," Xavier said. He straightened, tossing back a lock of hair from his face. "He was all mad this morning. Something about Picture Day."

"Manuel didn't come either," Levi said. "Told me he had some important experiment to do at home. You know Manuel." He shrugged, laughing.

Mr. J. Ar came up to the kids, beads of sweat still on his forehead from refereeing the game.

"Levi, you ready to go?"

"Sure, Dad, just a sec." He reached over to the table where he'd left his backpack.

"Mr. Arthur!" Mary Stanton, the college student who worked part time at the Rec, called from the door of the office, a phone in one hand, a coffee cup in the other. She insisted on calling Levi's dad "Mr. Arthur" rather than "Mr. J. Ar" like the kids did. "I need help in here!" Just then a child ran out of the office and jostled her, causing her to drop her coffee cup. She shrieked, abandoning the phone to save her chai latte.

"Coming, Mary," Mr. J. Ar said with a sigh. Mary was always in the middle of one crisis or another. "You kids hang tight. Brianna, you need a ride home?"

"That would be great, thanks."

As Mr. J. Ar went to deal with Mary Stanton's problem, Brianna's phone chirped. She pulled it from her hoodie pocket and looked at the screen. "It's a new message!" she exclaimed.

"It's not a message; it's just the Crest," Levi said. Then his phone made a beeping noise. He pulled it out of his backpack and looked at it. "I've got it too." The Crest appeared immediately, shining red in a black field.

"That's weird," Brianna said. "The Crest doesn't usually show up unless there's trouble. . . ." All three of them stood still, not knowing what to do, half expecting to be transported to Ahoratos instantly. But nothing happened. They were still at the Rec, holding their phones. Kids jostled around them to get their things and go outside to meet their rides.

"False alarm, maybe," said Xavier.

Brianna thrust her phone back into her hoodie pocket, disappointed. "Oh well. I guess we just have to wait a little longer."

"Can I borrow your phone?" Xavier asked Levi. "Evan's got mine. I need to text my dad, make sure he picks me up on his way home."

"Sure." Levi handed his phone to Xavier.

"It's so cute that you two have to share a phone," said Brianna.

"Actually, it's not," said Xavier. He took Levi's phone, closed out of the UNSEEN app, and began texting.

Suddenly all the lights in the building flickered and went out.

"What just happened?" Brianna asked. Around them kids hooted and giggled at the sudden darkness. Some used the light of their phones to find their way.

"Power outage," said Xavier, glancing around. "Good thing we're leaving. . . ." He looked down at the phone again, but instead of his message to his dad, the Crest of Ahoratos was glowing on the screen. "Hey, look at this," he said slowly, showing the phone to Levi. "The Crest came back."

"That's weird," said Levi.

Just then the image seemed to lift off the screen, hovering in the air before their eyes.

Brianna took out her phone and stared at it. "Mine's doing it too!" She watched as the Crest rose up from her phone screen. The two hovering Crest images soon began to shift toward each other, joining together in midair. They rotated, slowly at first, picking up speed.

"Just like the last time!" Brianna whispered. "Quick! Grab it!"

"The others will see us," Xavier said, looking around nervously.

"They aren't even looking!" Brianna retorted. "Besides, they can't see it. Only we can. Come on. Together!" She reached out toward the floating Crest. Xavier and Levi did too. Suddenly they felt as though they had just jumped onto a speeding merry-go-round, flung into motion, spinning so fast they couldn't see the room around them at all.

The lights flickered back on. Mary Stanton emerged from the office just as the three kids disappeared into thin air. She dropped her Starbucks. Again.

CHAPTER 6

The Infinity Space

Evan and Manuel gazed at the unending sea of whiteness around them. There was no landscape at all. Just empty, colorless space.

"Where are we?" Evan asked. "This doesn't look like Ahoratos. Usually there's—stuff. Trees and grass and stuff. It's like being inside a jar of cotton balls."

"Yes, very strange," Manuel answered in his scientific voice. He reached out tentatively to touch the whiteness around him. It felt very close, and yet he couldn't actually feel anything. "Invisible cotton balls." He bent down to see if there was a solid surface under his feet. There wasn't. "There is no earthly reason why we are still standing here and not falling through."

"No *earthly* reason," Evan said with a little chuckle. "Got that right."

"Of course we could be falling and not even know it, if we are in an area of microgravity."

"Micro-what?"

"Like astronauts in space—they look like they're floating, but they are actually falling at the same rate. . . ."

Evan knew Manuel was about to explain a bunch of stuff he didn't really want to hear about at the moment. So he interrupted: "Where is everyone else?"

Just then there was a noise, one Evan had heard once before—a noise like a garbage disposal trying to grind up a ham bone. And suddenly his brother Xavier was standing there too, along with Levi and Brianna. The three of them stared around, dumbfounded, blinking.

"Hey guys!" Evan said. "'Bout time you showed up."

"Evan?" said Xavier slowly, squinting, as if he didn't trust his own vision. "Manuel?"

"Where are we?" Brianna asked nervously.

"Ahoratos!" said Evan. "I mean, probably."

"There's no floor," said Xavier, bending to feel under his feet as Manuel had done. "What are we standing on?"

"Gravity," said Evan. "According to him."

"*Micro*gravity," said Manuel. "What I think happened is—"

"How do we get out of here?" asked Levi, interrupting.

"We need to find the Water," Xavier said, knowing that any delay in finding the Water could have disastrous consequences. Those were the instructions Ruwach had given them the first time they came to Ahoratos. They had to go through the Water in order to get to the Cave, where they could get their armor. It was dangerous to be in Ahoratos without their armor. Ruwach had told them that plenty of times.

"Yeah," said Evan, a tad nervously. His eyes darted around half expecting a sand grobel or bolt of lightning to strike like they had before.

"But . . . there's no Water here," Brianna said. "There's like—*nothing* here."

"Literally," said Levi.

"Maybe it's like the dome!" Evan said. "Remember the dome that Levi was trapped in? That was invisible."

"But it was still solid," Xavier said. "And we could still see the ground. I can't see anything through this white stuff except—more white stuff."

"Actually, we're *not* standing on anything—" Manuel tried to explain about the microgravity thing, but everyone continued to ignore him.

"We *really* need to find the Water," Evan said, more nervous.

"Maybe the Water is invisible," said Brianna.

"Then how are we going to be able to get into it?" Levi asked.

For reasons that Evan couldn't pinpoint, the mysterious instruction he'd received the day before floated across his mind like a waving banner:

Ask and it shall be given.

"Maybe we could just *ask* for it," Evan said.

"Ask?" Levi said, cocking an eyebrow at him. "For the Water?"

"Didn't you read the instruction from yesterday? 'Ask and it shall be given.' Maybe that's what it was talking about," Evan answered. "So—let's just ask."

He cupped his hands around his mouth and yelled up into the white blankness around them. "Ruwach, if you can hear me, please give us the Water!"

He expected to hear his own voice echo back to him, as it usually did in large places like this. But it actually sounded as though his voice just evaporated into space, or like it never even left his own mouth.

They waited, but nothing happened.

"No echo," said Manuel, mirroring Evan's thoughts. "That confirms my suspicions that wherever we are has no walls, no ending. It's like an . . . infinity space."

"Infinity space. Cool," said Levi, nodding his head thoughtfully. "Guess that means we aren't going to walk out of here." He let out a laugh, like he was making a joke. No one else thought it was funny.

"If there's no air, how are we breathing?" said Xavier.

"The fact that we are breathing means that there must be oxygen in the atmosphere," Manuel said.

"So where are we? We're not on earth, and maybe we're not even in Ahoratos—are we like . . . between the two?" Brianna asked. "Are we—stuck?"

"Yeah, like maybe the Crest-portal-thing ran out of gas or something," Levi said. He laughed again.

"I seriously doubt a portal would run out of gas," said Manuel, perfectly serious. "Still, it is not a very propitious situation for us at the moment."

"Pro . . . what?" said Evan, still disbelieving that an eleven-year-old would use a word like *pro-whatever-it-was* for goodness' sake.

"It means promising."

"Well why didn't you just say that?"

A new sound interrupted them, a sort of high-pitched squeal, like a rusty-hinged door opening. The kids stopped talking and looked up, as the sound seemed to be coming from somewhere above them. It was hard to tell, though, as sound in this place didn't reverberate—it died as quickly as it began.

"What is it?" Brianna whispered, searching the empty space above them for the source of the sound.

It was something. *Something.* Although they weren't sure quite what. The squeal seemed to be getting louder and closer until it—whatever *it* was—began to materialize before them. A transparent curtain of some sort, about five feet wide but extending so far above and below them that no end could be seen. The surface of the curtain appeared to be moving, rippling like a thin veil of water.

"Water! See?" Evan gloated. "Told ya."

"That's the Water?" Brianna asked, peering at it.

"Weird," said Lovi. "Kinda looks like water, but not really."

Manuel slowly reached out to poke it; his finger went right through. "It does feel like water," he concluded. "But it's very peculiar." He walked all around to the other side of the thing, scratching his head.

"Can you see me?" he asked.

"Sorta," Brianna said. "You look—wavy."

"Ah, interesting," Manuel said, coming back around to their side. "Some sort of visible wave form, perhaps, although it must be far more dense than it appears. . . ." Manuel began mumbling to himself, sorting out various hypotheses.

Evan had started walking around the strange, wavy curtain too. When he got to the other side, he poked his finger into it as Manuel had done. "Hey, look at my finger!" he said, wiggling it around.

"Where is it?" Brianna asked.

"You can't see it?" said Evan. "What about this?" He stuck his foot through "Can you see my foot?"

"Nope," said Xavier.

Evan pulled out his foot. It was completely dry. He came around to join the others again. "Cool. It must be the Water!"

"Well, I'm not so sure of that," Manuel said. "It seems designed to simulate water and therefore could be some sort of trap. Might just swallow us whole." A flicker of hesitation showed on his face. "I propose we study it further . . . I wish I had my microscope here, or at least a magnifying glass. . . ."

"There's the Crest! I can see it!" Levi pointed to the rippling curtain, where the funny-shaped א glowed very dimly.

"Wait. . . . I see it too!" Evan said. The others soon nodded in agreement. "That must be the Water!"

"There's only one way to find out for sure," Levi suddenly declared. He took a step right into the mirrorlike curtain. His leg disappeared just like Evan's had done. "See ya!" His voice was full of mischief as he stepped forward, the rest of him following and promptly disappearing altogether.

"Levi!" Brianna gasped. But he was gone before she could even try to pull him away.

"Where'd he go?"

Evan rushed around to the other side of the sheet to see if Levi would reappear there. But he didn't. "He must be—in there," he murmured. "Somehow . . ."

"Look!" Xavier said, pointing to the sheet, where a pale reddish tinge spread out from the center of the

Crest. Red. It was the hue that always spread across the surface of the Water when someone passed through its surface. This is what made it different from ordinary water.

"Definitely the Water," Brianna said, feeling suddenly secure that Levi was safely in the Cave. "See ya!" she chirped to the others as she nearly jumped into the rippling Water. She, too, disappeared.

"Hey, wait for me!" Evan shouted and dashed through the Water next. Xavier and Manuel were left.

"You want to go first?" Xavier asked.

"Perhaps we should wait a bit, just to make sure—"

"You can wait, if you want. But I'm going." Xavier stepped into the Water and disappeared with the others.

"Wait!" Manuel cried, but it was too late. Xavier was gone. Manuel remembered the last time he'd almost been left behind, when he'd been too scared to cross the bridge to Skot'os. He wasn't about to let that happen again.

He started counting, which was what he always did in scary situations. "One, two, three . . ." He stuck his foot into the Water. "Four, five . . ." He shut his eyes and lunged forward, disappearing completely before he could say, "six."

CHAPTER 7

The Corridor of Keys

Xavier blinked, gazing around him in relief. His friends were all there, wearing the armor they had been issued on their first visit—the white, triangular breastplate with the glowing orb in the center, the white, plain belt, and the tall boots. Their clothes had changed to the leatherlike gray pants and shirts as well.

Manuel appeared a few seconds later, also wearing his warrior clothes and armor. His eyes were still squeezed shut. He opened one and then the other, then let out a breath.

"This place looks different." He took off his glasses and put them in his pocket. His eyesight was always perfectly clear in Ahoratos.

They were in a long dark corridor, almost like the Hall of Armor where they'd first received their breastplates, belts, and boots. But they couldn't see any displays of armor. Instead, tall white pedestals of various heights surrounded them. On each pedestal rested a box—the boxes were of all different shapes and sizes, some very plain and some quite ornate. The boxes and their pedestals glowed brightly as if each were lit by its own spotlight.

"Are we even in the Cave?" said Evan.

"Must be," said Levi. "We came through the Water. But what's in all the boxes?"

"Let's see," said Evan, moving toward one. He was stopped in his tracks by the clear, unmistakable voice of Ruwach booming over his head.

"Welcome once again, young Warriors."

Ruwach was suddenly standing before them as if he'd just appeared out of nowhere—a small figure in a purple robe, his face hidden deep within the folds of his hood.

"Ruwach?" said Brianna. "Where are we?"

"In the Cave, of course. This is the Corridor of Keys." Ruwach spread his arms to indicate the boxes. "This is where we keep the keys of the kingdom."

"I thought there was only one key," said Evan, scratching his head.

"I never said there was only one." Ruwach's voice held a hint of mystery.

"So the key to our locked rooms is in here too?" Evan asked.

The locked rooms.

The first time they'd come to the Cave, the kids had seen the locked doors, one beside each set of armor. Ruwach had told them that the contents of the rooms belonged to them but that the key to the rooms had been stolen. Ponéros had deceived Rook into taking it in exchange for great riches; but once Ponéros had the key in his possession, he threw Rook into prison. The children had rescued Rook, but for all they knew, the key they needed—the key they longed for to open their locked rooms and finally see what was inside of them—was still in the enemy's possession somewhere in Skot'os. So every room was still shut tight, taunting the Warriors like a secret waiting to be told.

"That key is still in Skot'os," Xavier said. "Right, Ru? I mean, Ruwach?"

"I have retrieved it," Ruwach said. "The key to the locked rooms is here." The kids looked at each other, shock and surprise etched on their faces.

"So we get to open our rooms then?" Levi asked.

"That is not why you are here," said Ruwach.

The kids groaned in frustration. "Did you bring us in here just to tease us?" Evan said with a huff.

"No, Prince Evan. There is a time and season for all things. Today is not for keys. It is for shields." Ruwach reached out one long arm toward a box near him, one of the larger boxes that appeared to be covered in brownish-green vines and leaves. The box opened, although the kids didn't actually see Ruwach's fingers touch it. Inside was a key. It was the same color as the box and very curvy, as if it too were made of twisted vines. He lifted the key and motioned to the kids.

"You will need your shields now," Ruwach said. "The enemy is angry. You freed Rook, and Rook in turn has freed many others from the Fortress of Chaós. You will need further protection. Come. Follow me."

Ruwach turned and began moving toward the darkened end of the room. The kids hastened to follow, excited at the prospect of getting their shields. They had seen them the first time they'd come to Ahoratos, hanging on the wall along with the rest of their armor: majestic golden shields as tall as they were, slightly curved and emblazoned with the Crest of Ahoratos. Warrior shields.

Ruwach led them down several more dark tunnels, picking up speed as he went. The kids had to stay close so as not to run into a wall or trip over each other. The light from their breastplates cast a faint glow before them, as did the tiny purple lights that illuminated the passage wherever Ruwach headed. He took several turns and then picked up speed on a long straightaway. He was moving so fast now that the kids could hardly keep up with him.

"This reminds me of that night in the forest," Evan panted as they ran. "He's fast for a guy with such short legs."

"Who says he has legs?" said Levi. "I mean, have you ever seen any legs?"

Finally Ruwach stopped before a large ornate door—more like a gate—causing the kids to run into each other as they skidded to a halt. None of them spoke as Ruwach placed the key into the keyhole of the gate. It slowly swung open.

The first thing they heard was a low hum, like the rumble of an air conditioner in a very quiet room.

Ruwach moved much more slowly now, entering the new room, beckoning the kids to follow him. As soon as they did, they realized they were not in a room at all. They could see sunlight dripping in through a canopy of leaves overhead. Vines hung down from tall trees with long, curled branches and huge, teardrop-shaped leaves. The ground beneath them was not stone; it was hard-packed dirt.

"It's a garden," Brianna whispered. It was so quiet she couldn't bring herself to speak out loud. Eerily quiet, except for that weird, low hum. "Kind of a creepy garden though."

The masses of vines fell upon the kids' shoulders as they followed Ruwach down the path. Unlike the Cave, which felt mysterious and otherworldly, this place seemed much more real, more alive.

"Be careful," said Ruwach. "We are outside of the Cave now."

"It's like that place Mom took us in the city, remember Xavi?" Evan belted out, causing the others to cringe. "The mechanical garden?"

"*Botanical* garden," Xavier corrected in a hushed tone. "And yeah, it does kind of look like that."

"Why is everyone whispering?"

"Shhhh."

They followed the path around several tall trees with more vines hanging down, brushing the kids' faces and shoulders as they passed. The path was red, as if the soil itself was red. Not the usual brownish-red like clay, but bright red, ketchup colored. Blood colored.

A branch poked Brianna, and she jumped back, startled, rubbing the sting on her cheek.

"Sharp," she whispered. "That hurt." She reached out to push the vines and branches out of her way as she carefully stepped forward again. The others did as well, sensing that the plants around them were not particularly pleased by their presence.

They came to the end of the path, where a single tree stood unencumbered by vines or moss. This tree had long branches that dipped low into the ground. In fact, the branches actually grew right down into the red dirt.

"Never saw a tree do that," said Manuel, inching forward to study how the branches disappeared into the ground. "Must be its way of replanting itself—"

"You are correct, Prince Manuel," said Ruwach.

Ruwach crouched down under the tree. The kids saw his hands emerge from his sleeves; his long fingers glowed brilliantly, as if they were made of light. They had seen his hands a few times, but they still had never seen his face. Ruwach began to dig, sending sprays of scarlet dirt into the air, shimmering in the light from above. Specks of red dirt settled on their hair and skin so that the kids felt as if they, too, were coated in red.

Ruwach dug in silence. The kids tried to ask him questions about what he was doing, but he didn't answer.

After a while, they began to get antsy and wandered around, investigating the various plants around them.

Manuel was particularly enthralled, as there were species here even stranger than the ones he had in his room.

"This one looks like a skunk cabbage," Manuel said, pausing over a large, bulbous plant with a purple flower in the center. "But not quite." Then he came to another plant that had long curly stalks like corkscrews shooting straight up. "Could be a trachyandra! I've never seen one up close before. They can only grow in South Africa. I'd like to take a cutting back with me for my collection—"

"You can't take anything back with you, remember?" Brianna said. Another branch brushed the back of her head; she jumped, knocking her foot against something hard. She stooped to see what it was, pushing aside some tangled vines to reveal a large red stone. It hadn't been painted red, it *was* red. She'd never seen a stone this color before. When she touched it, the redness moved, like it was actually a fine covering on the stone. She shifted more of it aside until she had uncovered some writing engraved into it:

The Garden of Red

"Look!" she said, calling the others to see. They all looked at the red stone curiously.

Levi looked over his shoulder at Ruwach, who was only a short distance away but still quite involved in digging. "Maybe he will explain it," said Levi in a raspy whisper. "If he ever finishes digging." Ruwach continued his work, paying no attention to what the kids were saying. "Probably not," said Evan with a sigh.

"Red dirt," said Manuel, sticking his fingers in the dirt around the stone and rubbing them together. "Like Mars . . . or Oklahoma."

"This isn't Mars," said Xavier.

"And it sure ain't Oklahoma," Levi said with a laugh.

"There aren't any shields here," Evan said disappointedly. "I've looked."

"They're probably still back in the Hall of Armor, where the other pieces came from," said Brianna.

Evan was tempted to ask Ruwach about going to the Hall of Armor, but he had a feeling the guide still wasn't going to answer. Instead, he leaned toward Brianna and asked: "Why didn't Ruwach take us there instead of here? Maybe we're going there next. . . ." He turned back toward the gate where they'd entered, but it was gone. There was nothing but thick green vines where the doorway had been.

"We can't get out," Brianna whispered.

"Guess we'll have to wait to find out why Ruwach brought us here first," said Xavier.

They huddled closer together, watching their guide silently, growing more nervous the longer this went on.

"What's he digging for?" whispered Levi.

"Maybe he buried the shields here," said Brianna.

"Why would he bury the shields?"

"Who knows?" Xavier said. "To keep them safe, maybe. If Ponéros would steal the key, he might steal more stuff too."

"He'd need a much bigger hole to bury those big shields," said Evan.

"But Ponéros can't get into the Cave, can he?" said Brianna, wrinkling her nose.

"We aren't in the Cave, remember?" said Levi.

"It looks to me as though he's digging up one of those branches," Manuel said, peering at Ruwach.

Just then Ruwach rose, holding up one of the long, swaying tree branches. At the end of it there was something round and red—a deep, dark, crimson red.

Manuel moved closer to the red thing, his face clouded with skepticism.

"You must have faith, Prince Manuel." Ruwach responded to the question Manuel had not even asked.

"Faith?"

"Yes. Your faith is your shield."

"How can faith be a shield? That's impossible!"

"Nothing. Is. Impossible." Ruwach spoke each word as if it were a sentence in itself.

With that, he took the round, red thing in his two hands and slowly split it open, so that his Warriors could see what was inside.

The Garden of Red

CHAPTER 8

Seeds of Doubt

"What are they?" Levi asked. "Skittles?"

The kids peered with some dismay at the small, hard, red dots inside the cocoon-like thing Ruwach had opened.

To Evan and Manuel, they looked very familiar.

Manuel groaned. "Not those things again!" he said. "I thought we were getting real shields today!"

"How can Skittles be shields?" Brianna asked.

Manuel shook his head. "They aren't Skittles, they're *seeds*," he said. "Plain old boring seeds."

"You've seen them before?" Xavier asked.

"Yeah. My mom had one. These are exactly the same."

"Not exactly," Ruwach said, a sort of smile in his voice. "Similar, yes, but exactly, no. No two are ever alike."

"Well, they look the same," said Manuel.

"They definitely aren't shields," Evan said, crossing his arms.

"You must trust me, Prince Evan, Prince Manuel," Ruwach said, without a trace of impatience. "Hold out your hands."

Brianna stuck out her hand immediately. Xavier and Levi followed more slowly, Evan and Manuel, slower still. Ruwach placed one of the small red seeds in each of their palms.

Brianna held hers up to inspect it. "Shiny," she said, smiling a little. "Kind of pretty actually. Maybe I could make it into a necklace. . . ."

"Great," said Evan, rolling his eyes. "We come for shields and get jewelry."

"They're really . . . hard," said Xavier, trying to squeeze his between two fingers.

"What do we do with them?" Levi asked. "Plant them?"

"Take your seeds back to earth with you," Ruwach said. "Cultivate them. Protect them. Use them."

"I thought we weren't supposed to take anything from here?" Xavier said.

"This is different. Keep it with you at all times. How well you care for it will determine its power."

"But there *is* no power," Manuel said, irritated. "I've already checked. A thousand times. It doesn't *do* anything. . . ."

Just then one of the tall curly stalks near Manuel came to life. Its leafy tentacles became like long, sinewy fingers, reaching for Manuel's seed as if to snatch it out of his hand. Manuel jumped away, shocked at the aggressive behavior of a thing that was supposed to be mere vegetation.

"That plant just tried to attack me!" he yelped.

"Whoa! Like your Venus flytrap," said Evan. He felt something brush the back of his neck and whirled around to see a leafy vine slithering down his arm toward the seed in his hand. He closed his fist, snatching his hand away.

"It wants the seeds," said Xavier, gripping his seed and looking around for more attacking plants. "But what for?"

"There are many who would like to steal your seed," Ruwach said serenely. "Be on guard. Follow me."

Ruwach spun around and headed back down the winding path they'd taken to get to the tree with the weird branches. The kids quickly followed. As they moved through the garden more plants and vines came alive, twirling around their ankles and slinking down their arms, clearly attracted to the seeds within their hands. The trees leaned in toward them, their teardrop leaves stretching toward the tiny seeds. Brianna found she had to hold hers tight in both hands to make sure it wouldn't get snatched away.

"We need to get out of here," Brianna said. She jumped ahead, avoiding a tall tree that had started to bend toward her. The Warriors clustered together as the vines grew longer and thicker, snaking toward them.

As they neared the end of the path, they saw that the gate was still completely overgrown with thick, tangled vines.

"Hurry, Warriors!" Ruwach commanded as he approached the gate. He threw up his hands, and the vines suddenly untangled, withdrawing from the gate, which swung open creakily.

The kids barreled through the portal, which slammed shut behind them, as vines once again curled around the iron bars, still trying to reach the seeds.

"That's one crazy garden," Levi said under his breath.

"This way." Ruwach began to move again. "Keep up."

"Hopefully we will go to the Hall of Armor now and get the real shields," Evan muttered.

Ruwach led them back through the twisting tunnels, but instead of ending up in the Hall of Armor, they came again to the Corridor of Keys. Ruwach stopped to put the garden key back in its vine-covered box.

Evan turned his face toward Ruwach expectantly, waiting for something else. Something more. But Ruwach was still. "So that's it?" asked Evan, sounding annoyed. "This is all we get?"

"This is all you need," said Ruwach placidly. "Remember this: the enemy will do anything to stop you from using the seeds." Ruwach's voice dropped low, as if he were imparting some dreadful secret. "You must be careful."

"You mean we are in even more danger than before, just for having these?" Evan asked, his eyes wide with fear, his hand containing the seed stretched out toward

Ruwach. "Why are you giving us these things then? How about going and getting the real shields now . . . quit fooling around. . . ."

Xavier flicked him on the back of his head.

"Ouch!" Evan gasped.

"You do not have to be afraid, Prince Evan. Your seed *is* your shield." Ruwach reached out and patted Evan on the shoulder. Evan was not very comforted.

"But what about the shields we saw in the Hall of Armor?" Evan insisted. "They were big and strong. Why can't we have those? I mean, those are the shields that go with our armor. They were real shields! Not these dumb seeds—"

Xavier put a hand on Evan's shoulder to stop him from going further. But the other kids looked as though they agreed with Evan. They stared glumly at their little seeds, no one even trying to contradict Evan. Xavier knew he had to do something to keep them all on track. He turned to Ruwach.

"We'll do what you say," he said. "But it would help if . . . there was an instruction."

"Ah, yes . . ." Ruwach spread one arm toward the opposite end of the room. A pinprick of light appeared, flickering faintly, very far away. Ruwach drew his arm back, and as he did, the object grew brighter, closer, coming toward them at breakneck speed.

The kids didn't flinch, not even Evan. The Book sped toward them and then just as suddenly stopped, resting on its golden pedestal. The kids stared at it, once again amazed at its magnificence. It was very large, with a glowing cover from which the Crest of Ahoratos seemed to rise up like a 3-D image, twirling in the air. The Book, they knew, came from the Source—the source of all Life and Truth.

Ruwach lifted one arm, and The Book opened, the shining pages flipping quickly at first, then more slowly. As each page turned, it hummed, sort of like music, ringing out a different note. After a moment Ruwach dropped his arm, and the pages stopped flipping.

The kids leaned in for a better look. The Book had opened to a page that was full of strange characters and letters all scrambled up. Brianna thought it looked just like the images that often appeared on her phone. But Ruwach made another small gesture with his arm, and the letters lifted off the page, hovering in the air, flickering gently.

fI ehlt eodeett sehl vmuaa fsoa sitfhe ihzse loits in ebelp ymog hos bni frywuiol

"That's still so cool," Evan murmured. Xavier nudged him to be quiet.

Ruwach waved his arm again. Before their eyes, the letters rearranged themselves to form a sentence that glowed ever brighter:

If you have faith the size of the smallest seed, nothing will be impossible for you.

Ruwach suddenly raised both arms, grabbing the words out of the air and flinging them toward each of the children's breastplates. The orbs in the center of their breastplates spun and glowed, absorbing the instructions, the new words spinning around inside them.

"Wish I could believe it," Manuel murmured under his breath.

Ruwach's arms folded back into his robe once again. "Go now, Warriors, take care of your seeds."

"Wait . . . that's it?" Evan protested. "What about the battle? Don't we have a mission?"

"Take care of your seeds. . . ." Ruwach was fading from their vision, but his voice still resounded as if he were near. "That *is* the mission." In his place was a thin stream of light that seemed to pour in from the ceiling and bore down through the floor. The light gradually widened, revealing a white expanse like the one from which they'd come.

"Guess that's the way out," said Levi with a shrug. "Back through the white space." He was the first to walk through, disappearing into the light. Brianna and Xavier went as well, followed by Manuel, who was still staring at his seed and muttering to himself.

Evan glanced around the room one more time before setting foot through the open portal. There were dozens of boxes. One of them held the key to the special locked rooms. He was convinced that he and the others needed what was in those rooms to have real victory over the enemy, but still Ruwach wouldn't give it to them. That didn't seem fair at all.

His eyes fell upon a plain wooden box sitting on a simple pedestal with no engraving or ornamentation. He remembered back to when Ruwach had first shown them the empty box—it was just like this one. Plain and simple. He looked around but didn't see any other boxes that looked quite like it. This must be the one. He was sure of it. Amazing that he was able to see it so easily among so many other boxes.

He crept toward the box, hoping that Ruwach wasn't around to catch him. He opened it carefully. A key rested on purple satin lining. It was sort of skinny and rusted with an odd-shaped bow—a long shaft with four corkscrew crosspieces. It wasn't anything like the key they'd found in Skot'os—the one that had opened Rook's prison door. In fact, it was unlike any other key he had ever seen before. So this must be the key that opened the locked rooms. Evan wondered how Ruwach had managed to get it back.

Evan looked over at the glowing portal—his way back home—it was narrowing again. Pretty soon it would be gone completely. No time now. But the next time he got to the Cave, he knew what he would do.

He shut the box and ran quickly to slip through the crack of light before it sealed once again.

CHAPTER 9

Keeping Seeds

Evan sat on the edge of his bed, staring down at the red seed.

He'd put it in the drawer of his nightstand before going to bed, figuring that would be a safe enough place. But he couldn't sleep. For an hour he tossed and turned, unable to shake off the words of Ruwach: *"The enemy will do anything to stop you. . . . Many will try to take it from you. . . ."*

He finally just opened the drawer and picked up the seed, examining it closely, rubbing his thumb over the hard shell. It really did look like a Skittle. He raised it to his mouth and bit it, just to see if it might actually be candy. Maybe it was just Ruwach's idea of a joke, giving them candy instead of a real seed. The shell was so hard it hurt his teeth. Definitely not candy. He gazed at the seed, noticed he'd left a tiny tooth mark in the smooth surface. Maybe it wasn't as hard as he thought it was.

"Danger is on the way. . . . The enemy is angry. . . ."

Evan shut his eyes against the chilling words. He put the seed back in the drawer and slammed it shut. He had a sudden, terrible thought that the enemy might be in his very room, lurking in the shadows or—under the bed. He'd better check, just to be sure.

He got his flashlight out of the nightstand, got down on his knees, took a big breath for courage, and shined the light under the bed. No evil enemy. Just a lot of junk. His play armor, which he'd shoved under his bed a month ago, and the book. He'd forgotten about that book.

He reached under the bed and pulled it out, dusting off the cover. It was the book about the Prince Warriors, just like the one Manuel had. Evan's grandfather had given it to him years before, when he was too young to even read it. But he loved looking at the pictures of the mighty warriors riding horses and killing dragons. On the cover was the weird symbol he had come to learn was the Crest of Ahoratos. He ran his finger over the symbol. How strange was it that he had actually been to the place that this book told about. Weirder than weird.

He opened the book to the chapter about the shield. There was a picture of a Prince Warrior holding up a tall, curved shield emblazoned with the Crest of Ahoratos. It looked pretty much like the shield he had first seen in the Hall of Armor in the Cave. Evan looked closer, noticing something small and red embedded in the round metal boss at the center of the shield. It looked like a gem at first, maybe a ruby. But as he stared at it, he realized it also looked a lot like his seed.

He opened the drawer and took out the seed, placing it next to the picture of the shield in the book. It did look very similar. . . .

He shook his head, pushing the thought away. No, that was silly. No shield would be decorated with a seed. It had to be a fancy jewel of some sort. Something really valuable.

He put the seed back in the drawer. Then he closed the book and shoved it back under his bed. He lay back down and pulled the covers up to his chin, keeping the flashlight in one hand just to be on the safe side. He closed his eyes and tried to sleep again. But Ruwach's warning wouldn't go away.

"Danger is coming. . . ."

Evan sat up in bed, shaking. An Ent was in his room. He fumbled under the blanket for his flashlight and with shaking hands turned it on, aiming the beam at the chair. He hoped that would scare the Ent away.

But it wasn't an Ent. It was his jacket and baseball cap, which he'd thrown on the chair when he was getting ready for bed.

Evan lay back down, his heart hammering so hard in his chest he could feel it in his ears. He tried to calm himself down.

Only a jacket. Not an Ent . . .

He saw a long, dark shadow move on the ceiling. He pulled the covers over his head. After a while he peeked out. Only a shadow. Or was it? How was he to know which shadows were just ordinary shadows and which were—the enemy?

Evan lay in the dark, thinking about the trouble this little seed was creating. He couldn't see how it could ever help him. It might even be a kind of homing device, showing the enemy exactly where he was.

He had to get rid of it, or he'd never get any sleep ever again.

He opened the drawer and picked up the seed. He got up, threw a hoodie over his head, and padded downstairs as quietly as he could. He went to the kitchen and opened the back door slowly enough that the squeaks in the hinges wouldn't wake his mom. She had eagle ears to match her eagle eyes.

The night air was very cool, and Evan shivered as he stepped out onto the back porch. Moonlight flickered on the pond and dappled the leaves of the trees. Regular trees, he saw. Not twisted black trunks, like the first time he'd been called to Ahoratos. He glanced back at the house to make sure it was still there—the windows, the doors, the chimney. It was. He breathed a sigh of relief. He tiptoed down the steps to the grass and made his way to the huge rotted stump by the pond. This stump used to be a great old oak tree that had been split in two by lightning on the same night he and Xavier had gone to Ahoratos for the first time. He missed that old tree. It was great for climbing, plus it had a tire swing, which Evan had swung on for hours when his family first moved to this house in the country. His dad had attached the tire to a different tree, but it wasn't quite the same.

Evan turned toward the pond and stepped gingerly onto the dock, listening to the sounds of the night—crickets, soft breezes, the water lapping the shore and knocking the old rowboat this way and that. He looked out onto the dark water as it rippled gently, each ripple glinting in the moonlight. He gripped the seed tightly, shut his eyes, and threw it as far as he could into the pond. He heard a tiny "kerplunk" and opened his eyes, relieved it was gone. He felt safer now.

"Take care of your seed."

Ruwach's words suddenly rolled in his head, as if the little guide were speaking directly to him from some unseen place.

Well, I did take care of it, Evan thought to himself. *I did the only sensible thing.*

He hurried to the house without looking back, hoping that now he'd finally be able to get some sleep.

———

Xavier was awake as well, sitting on the edge of his bed. He'd heard his brother leave his room but just assumed he was going to the bathroom. Xavier held his seed and gazed around the room. He had to figure out a safe place to keep it. It was so small—he was afraid he would lose it if he just left it on his desk or under his pillow. He figured Ruwach was trying to test them, to see how obedient they could be. Xavier always tried to be obedient.

He picked up a dirty shirt from the floor and wrapped the seed in it. Then he got up and pushed it onto the top shelf of his closet, behind some shoe boxes. No one would see it there, not even his mom. And it would be safe. A burglar would never bother looking at an old, dirty shirt. He yawned, suddenly sleepy. Going back to bed, he lay down on his side so he could keep an eye on the closet until he fell asleep.

———

Levi was almost asleep when he remembered the seed. Where had he put it? He sat up, suddenly panic-stricken that he'd already lost it.

He was pretty sure he knew what Ruwach was up to. He was just making sure the kids could be responsible with this small, insignificant seed before he let them have the real shields. They were just kids, after all, and kids had a tendency to lose things. The other pieces of armor—the breastplate, the boots, and the belt—had to be worn, so they were a lot harder to lose. But the shield would be different. When they finally did get it, they'd pick it up to use it and put it down when they weren't using it. They would have to prove that they could handle such a responsibility before they were entrusted with anything so valuable as a shield from Ahoratos.

Levi did have a habit of losing things. It wasn't on purpose; it was just that he would get busy and forget.

He'd lost his phone once and had to work at the rec center for a month cleaning floors before his dad got him another one. That had really made him think twice before setting his phone down just any old place. Then there was that business with misplacing his boots during his first trip to Ahoratos, something he didn't even want to think about. But that tiny seed was so much smaller than either his boots or a phone, so much easier to lose.

Levi jumped out of bed and rooted through his backpack, checking all the different zippered pockets until he finally found the seed, nestled in the very bottom. He pulled it out and wiped off the pencil shavings that were stuck to it. There was some other stuff in the bottom of his backpack that he'd forgotten about: a smooshed Snickers bar, a broken pencil, and a bunch of pennies. Sometime he really needed to clean that backpack out.

He found a pencil case and unzipped it, dumping out all the stubby pencils and gum wrappers. Then he stuck the seed into the case and zipped it closed. As long as he kept it there, he didn't have to worry about losing it. Satisfied, he went back to bed.

———————

Brianna pulled a plastic bin from under her bed. It contained lots of ribbons and sequins and gemstones, the things she used to make her own headbands. She found a little container of stick-on jewels, then slipped the bin back under her bed.

She heard one of her sisters mumble. She froze . . . but then relaxed. Crystal talked in her sleep all the time. Mostly she sang bits and pieces of random songs she liked to listen to.

"Can't . . . stop . . . dreaming about you . . ." Crystal was actually singing now. Brianna stifled a giggle, waiting until Crystal finished her song and was quiet again. Nikki, her middle sister, was snoring loudly. Her oldest sister, Winter, always slept with her headphones on so she wouldn't be able to hear the snoring or the sleep talking.

Brianna took a small empty jewelry box from her dresser drawer and set about sticking on the multicolored fake jewels. She used small red ones to form a heart shape on the lid, then added silver ones around the outside for extra sparkle. On the sides she used alternating silver, red, and gold gems, sticking them on with little dabs of tacky glue. Soon the entire box was completely bedazzled. When she was done, she lifted the box up to the window so she could see the jewels glimmer in the moonlight. There, that was much prettier. She put the seed into the box and closed the lid. Then she got back into bed, slipping the box under her pillow, and went to sleep.

––––––––––

Manuel set the little red seed under the microscope. He adjusted the knobs, peering in the viewfinder until it came into focus. He couldn't see how it was different from his mother's seed at all. It looked exactly the same.

He took it out from under the scope and set it on his desk. He picked up a utility knife and tried to cut the seed in half. He thought if he could look inside. . . . He hadn't wanted to damage his mother's seed, in case his father should notice. But this one was Manuel's, so he could do whatever he wanted, right? He held the seed steady and pushed the tip of the knife into its shiny red surface. The seed's outer shell was so hard the knife just slid off the side, leaving a faint scratch mark. Manuel tried again and again, to no avail. More scratches.

"¿Manuel, qué pasa?" His father's voice echoed up from his study downstairs. Manuel's dad stayed up late most nights, in his study with the door closed. But he insisted Manuel be in bed with lights out at a "decent hour." That had been his mother's term. Times like this he missed his mother most—when he was staying up too late and she would come into his room, take the book or the paper or the lab experiment out of his hands, and make him go to bed. She knew he'd stay up all night, especially if there was something he needed to figure out. He wished she were here now, so he could ask her about the seed.

"Nada, papá!" Manuel called down. "Un minuto más!" He hooked the seed up to the electrodes as he had done for his mother's seed. This one was newer; maybe it still had some detectable electromagnetic activity. He tested it several times. Nothing happened. He finally gave up.

The lights in his room flickered off and then on again. Strange, he thought. That had happened the last time he was experimenting on the seed. But then again, he was always experimenting when he was in his room. And they lived on a country road with exposed electric wires, which were constantly getting blown around in the wind.

Manuel unhooked the seed and picked it up. Useless, he thought again. Completely useless.

This thing could never protect him from the enemy. He'd seen the work of that enemy up close. He'd been pretty scared the last time.

How could a seed be a shield anyway? That was just it. It couldn't. What if it was just supposed to plant an idea in his brain—an idea! Seed . . . plant! That was it! Ruwach gave them useless seeds in order to plant ideas in their minds about how they could create a real shield—one that would *really* protect them.

Manuel knew just what he was going to do. He would build his own shield! One that would be able to stop arrows and sword blows and maybe even bullets.

"¡Manuel, a acostarse!" Manuel's father shouted, more aggravated. "Get to bed now!"

"Okay, papá!" Manuel called back. He jumped up and went to the bathroom, setting the seed down on the counter so he could brush his teeth. When he was done he looked at the seed and shook his head. "Guess I don't need you anymore."

He turned toward the toilet and tossed it in.

And then, he flushed.

CHAPTER 10

An Old Friend

The last bell rang, and Levi picked up his coat and skateboard from his locker then went to catch the bus to the Cedar Creek Recreational Center. Every day seemed longer than the last. He didn't mind school that much, he just wished it wouldn't take so long.

He was excited about going to the Rec today because Xavier had asked him to show him some new skating tricks. It took a lot for Xavier to give up a day of basketball to skateboard with him.

When he jumped onto the bus, he saw Brianna in the seat in front of Xavier, facing backward on her knees to talk to him.

"Hey," Levi said, sitting down beside her. She turned around in the seat and smiled at him.

"Hi, Levi!"

"Hey," Xavier said with his customary head nod. Levi nodded back.

"Ready to skate?" Levi said.

"Sure," said Xavier. "I don't have a board though."

"No worries. We have plenty at the Rec. We'll do some noseslides today," Levi said. "Start with some simple stuff."

"Uh—okay," said Xavier. "Just go easy on me."

Brianna nudged Levi and opened her backpack to show him her seed in its bedazzled case.

"What do you think?"

Levi shook his head, laughing. "Figures."

"You got yours?" She leaned in closer, expecting him to open up his backpack too.

But he didn't offer.

"Yeah, I got it. Somewhere." He'd totally forgotten about the seed until that moment. But he hadn't taken it out of the backpack, so he was sure it was still in there. It had been six days since they'd gone to Ahoratos, and not a word had come from Ruwach. Levi had started to wonder if keeping the seed was even worth it at all.

"What about you?" Brianna asked Xavier.

"It's at home," Xavier said.

Brianna's voice became a hoarse whisper. "Ruwach told us to keep it with us all the time!" she said.

"Yeah, well, I didn't want it to get lost. I figured it would be safer at home."

Brianna made a "tsk tsk" noise with her tongue. "You're gonna get in tro-uble. . . ." she said, dragging out the last word so it sounded like two.

"No, I'm not," Xavier said. "Besides, it's just a little seed. It doesn't do anything."

"Ruwach said it was a shield," Levi said. "What do you think he meant by that?"

"No idea," said Xavier.

"I wish we'd gotten real shields," Levi said. "Or at least gotten whatever is in our locked rooms."

"What do you suppose is in there anyway?" Brianna asked.

"More weapons, maybe," said Levi. "Or jet packs. Or invisibility cloaks. Or turbocharged skateboards!"

"Exploding pens," said Xavier, laughing.

"A rocket-propelled bicycle!" said Brianna.

For the rest of the bus ride, they continued thinking up extravagant ideas of what could be hidden in their locked rooms.

Evan was standing in front of the rec center when the bus pulled up to the curb. "Where's Manuel?" he asked as his friends piled off.

"Don't know. Probably went home," Levi said. "He said he had a big project he was working on. He's being all secretive about it." He shook his head. "Manuel's really upset about the whole seed thing."

"Don't you think it's weird that his mom had the exact same seed?" Brianna said.

"Manuel told me the seed comes from South America, where his mom was from," Evan said. "So that's probably where she got it. Maybe people there collect them, for some reason."

"But why would Ruwach give us the same seed?" asked Brianna.

"Who knows what Ruwach is up to half the time," said Evan with a big sigh. "That guy is so confusing."

"You're just easily confused," Xavier said, punching his little brother on the shoulder playfully. "It makes perfect sense to me. This is a test."

"That's what I think too," Levi said. "He gave us the seeds to see if we'd be responsible with them or lose them."

"Yeah, and to see if we will really trust him," Xavier added. "Remember all the crazy instructions we got the last time? Like walking into the sandstorm?"

"And going into the Fortress of Chaós," said Brianna.

"You'd think just one time we could get an instruction that made sense," Evan said, throwing up his hands. He was thinking of how he'd tossed his seed in the pond. He wondered if he should have done that. He certainly hadn't followed Ruwach's—or The Book's—instructions.

Mr. J. Ar came out to greet the kids, giving each one a high-five and asking how their day had gone.

"We're going to skate today," Levi told his dad, indicating Xavier.

"Oh, really?" said Mr. J. Ar, glancing at Xavier, who shrugged. "Fine by me. But I've got a game starting in five minutes, so I'd better get going."

The kids followed Mr. J. Ar into the building. Levi stopped when he saw an old, rusty pickup truck pulling into the parking lot. It had the words "Creekside Landscaping" in white lettering on the driver's door. A young man got out, tall and lanky with sandy hair. He reached around to the bed of the truck and pulled out a chainsaw and some other tools.

Levi stared at the man a long time.

He looked familiar.

"Levi, what's up, man?" Xavier called from the doorway. "You coming?"

"Hold up," Levi said. He started walking toward the man, who was headed toward a large broken limb hanging from a nearby tree.

"Hey!" Levi shouted, breaking into a trot. The man was walking away from him and didn't hear. *It has to be him*, Levi thought. He'd know that guy anywhere. "Guys, look! It's him!" he called back to his friends as he ran.

Brianna looked closely at the man Levi was headed toward and then broke into a wide smile. "It is!" she said. "Come on, you guys!"

"Who is it already?" said Evan, annoyed. But he and Xavier followed after Brianna, who was sprinting after Levi.

"Rook!" Levi called out. The man turned and looked at him, recognition mixed with wariness in his face.

"Levi?" Rook smiled broadly and gave a little wave. He looked different from the last time Levi had seen him, in the courtyard of the castle in Ahoratos. For one thing, he no longer had any metal parts. He was wearing old jeans and a Creekside Landscaping T-shirt smeared with dirt. He had a scruffy beard, and his longish hair was in a ponytail.

"Yeah, it's me," Levi said with a shy smile. "What are you doing here?"

Rook set down the chainsaw as the kids gathered around to greet him. "I work for this landscaping company now," he said.

"But I thought you were in some kind of trouble. I mean, since you were a prisoner. . . ."

"I was. But I'm free now." He paused. "And I got this job, thanks to Mr. Blake."

"Our dad?" Xavier said, confused. "How do you know our dad?"

"Well, when I took down that oak tree in your backyard. . . ."

"*You* did that?" Evan said, remembering how the tree had to be cut up and cleared away after it'd been struck by lightning. He had no idea that it had been Rook.

"Yeah, well, it was part of my community service. But I guess I did a good enough job. Because of your dad's recommendation, this company was willing to take a chance on me."

"Crazy," said Levi with a grin. "I mean—that you would get hired by Mr. Blake after we rescued you from—you know. Do you think Ruwach might have had something to do with that?"

"It's certainly possible," said Rook with a wide grin.

"Stellar," Brianna said. "So, have you been back to . . . you know where?"

"You mean—there?" Rook said with a knowing smile. "Sure. A few times. Helping Ruwach with some special operations—"

"Special ops!" said Evan. "Cool! So you're like this ex-criminal-turned-special-ops-warrior-chainsaw-wielding landscaper. Epic."

They all laughed at that.

"I'll bet Ru had it all planned that way," Evan said. "I mean, that we would meet you here, after what happened in you-know-where."

Rook shrugged. "Ru is always pretty mysterious, that's for sure."

There was an uncomfortable lapse in the conversation as they all searched for the right words. There was really only one thing they wanted to talk about.

Ahoratos.

"We went back to . . . *there*," Evan started. "But all we got were some lousy seeds."

"Oh, the seeds," Rook said with a nod. His eyes lit up in the slightest way.

Evan's eyebrows furrowed. "They're useless, *and* they make us even more of a target for the enemy."

"Oh no, they're anything but useless."

"What do you mean?"

"You'll see. I need to get to work. But maybe we can talk more later—"

They were interrupted by the sound of multiple phones beeping with incoming messages. Levi, Brianna, and Xavier pulled out their phones and opened the screens at the same time.

"Is it Ruwach?" said Evan, jumping up to see what Xavier was looking at.

"It's Manuel," Brianna said, disappointed.

"Says we need to come to his house," said Levi. "He has something to show us."

"Now?" said Evan. "I mean, we just got here! And it's not raining, so we can hang out outside for once! And Rook is here! Tell him that."

Levi texted Manuel back and waited for a response. His phone beeped again. "He says it's really important."

"He's probably doing some crazy new experiment on that seed," Evan said, shaking his head. "Let's just stay here and skate. If it's so important, Manuel should just come here and show us."

"You okay, Evan?" Rook asked, a look of concern on his face.

"Sure, why?"

"You seem—upset about something."

"I'm not upset," Evan replied, turning away so Rook couldn't see his face.

"Let's go ask Mr. J. Ar," Xavier said. "Maybe he can give us a ride to Manuel's house."

Levi and Evan both groaned. Levi was really looking forward to skating with Xavier—or maybe he was looking forward to showing off for Xavier. He always felt that Xavier was slightly better than he was at most things, so it made him happy when there was at least one thing he could do better than Xavier.

Mr. J. Ar watched the kids approach with his arms crossed over his chest. Rook picked up his chainsaw and slung it over his shoulder. He nodded to Mr. J. Ar, who nodded back but didn't smile.

"What's up?" said Levi's dad, looking dubiously at them.

"We'd like to go to Manuel's house," Xavier said in a conspiratorial whisper. "It's kind of important."

"Manuel's house, huh?" said Mr. J. Ar. "Well, I can't take you. I need to ref the basketball game. But I suppose you could ask Mary to drive you."

"Miss Stanton?" Brianna said, alarmed. "But she's . . . you know . . ." Brianna didn't want to say what she thought of Miss Stanton. "Does she even know how to drive?"

"Yes, she has a license and everything. I'll give her the keys to my truck," Mr. J. Ar said, ignoring Brianna's objections. "You kids wait here."

CHAPTER 11

A Better Shield

Mary Stanton drove Mr. J. Ar's huge SUV like it was a tank, creeping along the state road at twenty-five miles per hour, forcing a line of cars to crawl behind her. She whipped her head around nervously, nearly knocking Xavier out with her long, blond ponytail.

"I've never driven anything this big before," she said in a panicky voice. Every time a car passed, she swerved to the right and ran over the rumble strips, making the kids cringe. "Sorry!" she kept saying.

"Not sure this was the best idea my dad ever had," Levi muttered.

When the SUV finally pulled into the driveway of Manuel's house, the four kids jumped out as fast as they could.

"Thanks, Mary," Levi said, although he didn't actually mean it.

"No problem!" Mary answered. Once all the kids were out, she put the SUV in reverse and slowly backed out of the driveway, stopping every couple of seconds to check her mirrors.

"That's gonna take a while," said Xavier, watching her struggle. "She might still be here when we get back." He laughed and headed up the sidewalk.

Evan looked up at the window of Manuel's room, thinking there might be some weird flashing going on like the last time. But he couldn't see anything. He followed the others to the front door.

Xavier rang the doorbell, and a minute later Manuel came to the door, breathless and flushed with excitement.

"Good thing you're here!" he said in a rush. "Wait till you see what I made!" Manuel darted up the stairs, Brianna and Levi close on his heels.

Evan paused. The door to Mr. Santos's study was slightly ajar again, like it had been the first time he'd come to the house. But he was pretty sure Mr. Santos wasn't home so—

He crept toward the door and opened it, peeking inside. Still lying on the desk was the book that had looked so familiar to him. He slipped through the door and inched toward the book, being careful not to touch anything.

"Evan. What are you doing?" Xavier said from the doorway.

Evan jumped, startled. His heart hammered in his chest as he tried to relax.

"Uh . . . look, Xavi. This book. There's something about it . . ." He was standing right beside it now, and as he peered down onto the opened pages he knew immediately why he'd been drawn to it in the first place. His eyes widened.

"Xavi, it's like my book, the one Grandpa gave me. The Prince Warrior book. With the Crest on the cover." Now he touched it lightly. Somehow he felt like he could, as if having one of his own gave him unspoken permission. "This one looks different. . . ." Evan said thoughtfully as he leafed through a few pages and then closed the book, examining the cover.

"So what's the big deal? Manuel told us he had one."

"This isn't Manuel's. His is in his room. I saw it there before, and it looked exactly like mine. But something isn't right about this one." Evan bent over and squinted his eyes, tilting his head to the side to look even more closely. And then, he saw it plain as day.

"Look—the Crest looks different here, like it's upside down or backward or something. And it's the wrong color. . . ." Evan's voice had risen with excitement. Xavier motioned for him to lower his voice as he turned around to check that they were still alone. Then he leaned closer to see for himself. Evan was right. The crest did look different from the one they'd come to know so well.

"Come on, Evan. Don't be nosy." Xavier pulled Evan away from the book and back to the door. Evan sighed and followed his brother out of the study, up the stairs, and down the hallway to Manuel's room.

Manuel stood in front of his bedroom door, waiting patiently until his entire audience was gathered. When Evan and Xavier finally arrived, Manuel threw open the door with a flourish:

"Ta-da!"

They stared, openmouthed, at the huge object leaning against the desk in the center of the room.

"What do you think?" Manuel asked, his voice practically squeaking with anticipation.

The kids looked at each other and then back at the colossal metal structure in front of them.

"What is it?" Brianna said, her mouth dropping open in wonder and awe.

"It's a shield!" Manuel said, annoyed that they couldn't see that for themselves. "I made it!"

"Whoa," said Evan, moving into the room for a closer look.

"You . . . made a shield?" said Xavier.

The thing was as tall as Manuel, made of several hubcaps welded together in a circular pattern. It was outlined in white rope lights, the Crest of Ahoratos hand-painted in bright red in the center.

"It's shiny," said Brianna.

"It's big," said Levi.

"This is so cool!" Evan exclaimed, running a hand over the shiny steel hubcaps. "Coolest shield I ever saw! How'd you make it?"

Manuel grinned, pleased that at least one of them was catching on. "Well, I thought about that seed a long time, and I finally decided that Ruwach never meant for us to actually use the seed as a shield."

"How do you know that?" said Xavier, folding his arms.

"Because—it just didn't make sense. Giving us a useless seed and calling it a powerful shield. I decided that the seed was symbolic." He paused proudly, lifting his eyebrows and smiling—waiting for agreement from the others. Instead, they all stared blankly. "Ruwach wanted to *plant* an idea in our minds. You get it? Seed? Plant?" They stared. Manuel realized that he was going to have to explain his theory after all. "The seed was just for inspiration. He really wants us to use our own ingenuity to come up with the shield. You know how tricky Ruwach can be sometimes."

"Yeah, but—" Levi began, but Manuel kept on talking.

"So I started searching the Internet for ideas. And that's what made me think of the hubcaps. I had my dad drive me to the junkyard. It was a little tough finding real steel hubcaps—most new cars don't have them anymore. But I managed to find a few and simply welded them together. Then I added some other parts—mostly pieces of steel frames I found—to make it stronger. I figured, the bigger the better, right? I bolted on handles from a car door. See? This thing will stop arrows, swords, even bullets!"

"You're a genius!" said Evan. The others began to nod, as if they agreed.

"It's . . . impressive. That's for sure," said Levi.

"Looks heavy," said Xavier.

"It is a bit too heavy, I'm working on that part." Manuel picked up the shield by the handles, but it was so heavy he could hardly get it off the floor. Evan rushed in to help.

"Big enough for two!" Evan said.

"Looks like you need two to carry it," said Xavier under his breath.

"Did you draw the Crest yourself?" Brianna said, eyeing the design critically.

"It was a rush job, I admit, but this is just the prototype. If I can find some aluminum alloy it will be a lot lighter but still pretty strong. Or better yet, titanium! Once I find some more hubcaps, I can make one for each of us!" Manuel said proudly. "A real shield! Try it out! Throw something at me!"

"Like what?" said Levi, looking around the room.

"How about the geodes?" Evan said, pointing to the crate on the floor.

"Geodes?" Levi asked.

"They're rocks with crystals inside. Pretty cool."

"What if they break?" Xavier asked.

"That's okay, I've got plenty," said Manuel.

Xavier picked up one of the geodes and tossed it from hand to hand. "Heavy," he said.

He took aim like a baseball pitcher and threw the geode as hard as he could. It made a wicked noise and put a tiny dent near the top of the shield before it bounced off and rolled on the floor.

"See?" said Manuel proudly.

"But what are you going to do with it?" Levi asked. "I mean, it's not like you can take it to school."

"I could take it to the Rec," said Manuel. "That way, if anyone tries to attack me—or any of us—I'll be ready."

"Attack us?" said Xavier doubtfully. "Who would attack us at the Rec?"

"I don't know. . . . Somebody might! Ruwach did say something about the enemy being even angrier than before," said Manuel. "And if he did attack, this would be a lot more useful than that ridiculous seed."

"Manuel's right. Ruwach said we would need to be prepared," said Evan. "The enemy *is* going to attack."

"I thought he meant in Ahoratos," said Levi.

"We could be attacked here as well as in Ahoratos," Manuel said. The idea of an attack on earth had never occurred to the Prince Warriors. Their heartbeats quickened at the thought. They knew that the battles they faced in Ahoratos affected their lives on earth, but they had never considered the possibility of the enemy waging war against them *here*.

Manuel didn't seem to notice the tension. "I might even be able to take this with me to Ahoratos the next time we go."

"I don't think it will go through," said Xavier.

"It might, if I hold on to it really tight," said Manuel.

"That's cool how you made the Crest light up," said Brianna. "How did you do that?"

"Light up?" Manuel wrinkled his nose. "I didn't make it light up."

"Then what's it doing?"

They all stared at the shield. The hastily painted-on Crest was actually glowing, as if it were lit up in neon. And then it seemed to peel away from the shield itself, floating above their heads.

Evan nearly jumped in the air. "It's the real Crest! Maybe we'll get to try out the shield right away!"

"Let's go," Levi said.

"Wait!" Brianna said. "The seeds! We need the seeds!" She rummaged through her backpack until she found her seed, still in its bedazzled case. Levi also delved into his backpack until he came up with his.

Xavier didn't have his with him. "Mine's in my closet at home. Just wait a minute, I'll go and get it. It's right across the street. Evan, you want me to get yours too?"

"Uh . . . no," said Evan, shaking his head. "I don't . . . have mine anymore."

The others looked at him.

"Did you lose it?" Brianna asked.

"Sort of," said Evan. "I kind of . . . threw it away."

"Threw it *away*?" said Brianna, incredulous.

"In . . . the pond."

"You threw your seed in the pond?" Xavier asked, shaking his head.

"So did I," said Manuel, although he didn't sound sad about it at all. "Not in the pond, of course. I flushed it down the toilet. But this shield is way better. Just stick with me, Evan. I'll keep you safe."

"Look, it's fading!" Levi said, pointing to the Crest. "We've got to go now!"

"I need to go get my seed," said Xavier. "You guys go without me, I'll catch up!" He dashed out the door and down the stairs.

"We should wait for Xavier," Brianna said. "But the Crest might be gone by the time he comes back. . . ."

"If Ruwach wants him there, the Crest will find him," said Levi. He gripped his seed in one hand and grabbed the Crest with the other. Brianna did too, closing her eyes. Manuel and Evan both held tightly to the homemade shield as they reached up to grab the Crest with their free hands. Instantly they felt as though they were being sucked into a giant vacuum, the room spinning around them like water going down a drain.

CHAPTER 12

Left Behind

Xavier burst in the back door of his house and raced up the stairs to his room. He knew he had to hurry. He headed straight for his closet, where his seed was still wrapped in a shirt. Unfortunately, over the last several days he'd thrown a whole lot of other clothes on that shelf as well, so it took some time to sort through it all to find the one that contained the seed. He unwrapped it, sighing in relief. The seed seemed to be glowing faintly. That was new.

"Xavier? What are you doing? I thought you texted me and said you were going to Manuel's house?" Mom's voice called from the hallway. "Is everything all right?"

"Sure, Mom," said Xavier, stuffing the seed in his jeans pocket. He dashed toward the door but found his way to the stairs blocked by his mother, who was holding a laundry basket. "I just . . . had to get something," he explained. "See you at dinner!" He brushed by her quickly and headed down the stairs.

"Wait!" Mom called out. Xavier stopped at the bottom step, groaning inwardly. "While you're here, would you do me a favor and run down to the basement and grab a few jars of tomatoes? I'm going to make some sauce for dinner."

"Um . . . can I do it later? I mean, I'm kind of in a hurry. . . ."

"No, Xavier. I need it now. It will only take a minute!"

"But Mom . . ."

"Do as your mother says."

Startled, Xavier whirled around to see his father sitting in his favorite chair in the living room, his laptop perched on his outstretched legs like it usually was whenever he was working from home. Xavier hadn't even noticed him sitting there when he hurried past earlier. He automatically straightened up at the sight of his father. It was something of a natural reflex.

"Your mother should never have to ask you the same question twice, son."

"Yes, sir," Xavier responded respectfully. He raced down the hall to the basement door and flew down the stairs; it wasn't until he got there that he realized he had no idea where his mom kept the jars of tomatoes. *Great*, he muttered to himself. *While the other kids are having adventures in Ahoratos, I'll be hunting for tomato jars.*

He pulled the cord of the single bulb light overhead and started making his way into the dark, unfinished basement. His dad had plans to fix it up as a game room for Xavier and his brother "someday," but he'd been so busy with work since they'd moved in that the project seemed to have been forgotten.

The basement gave Xavier the creeps. It was more like a cellar, with dank concrete walls that smelled funny. It reminded him an awful lot of the prison under the Fortress of Chaós.

He rummaged through a bank of cabinets that held old games, camping gear, Christmas decorations, and some stuff for making candles, from back when his mom had been interested in candle making. No tomatoes. He passed by a stack of boxes; one of them was labeled "Xavier's first year," full of mementos like his first tooth and a lock of hair from his first haircut. *Gross*. He had no idea why his mom saved that stuff.

Finally, he came upon a shelf that had rows of odd-colored vegetables marinating in jars—like a mad scientist's lair, he thought to himself, laughing a little. He looked for the red ones—but there were quite a few different kinds. He wasn't sure which were tomatoes and which were something else—like peppers.

He picked one of the jars off the shelves and examined it. He saw tiny seeds, which could be tomato seeds. It reminded him of the seed in his pocket. He glanced down to make sure it was still there and gasped. His whole pocket was glowing, like it was on fire. He felt his heart race—was the seed going to burn right through his pocket? He reached in tentatively and pulled out the seed. It was warm, but not too hot, and glowing very brightly, bathing all the jars on the shelves in an eerie red light. Xavier blinked several times, wondering if he was imagining all of this.

Before he could even think about what to do with the glowing seed, one of the jars fell off the shelf and crashed onto the concrete floor at his feet. Xavier jumped back, startled. Had he done that? Now there was a big mess of shattered glass and tomato goop on the floor. He'd have to get something to clean it up. But before he could move, he heard a soft rumble and the gentle clanging of glass jars. He looked to see that the shelf itself was shaking. He reached out to steady it. But the shaking just got worse.

Was it an earthquake? He pushed the seed back in his pocket so he could use both hands to steady the shelves. A jar fell; Xavier caught it and tried to put it back, but soon another jar fell, slipping through his fingers. It hit the floor, splattering glass shards and icky vegetables all over him.

"Mom!" he called out. He needed to warn her about the earthquake. As more jars lost their balance, he abandoned the shelf and turned to head for the stairs. The light went out. He wondered if the lightbulb had been shaken out of its socket. He was in complete darkness.

The rumbling continued. Xavier took out his phone and turned on the flashlight icon so he could see what was going on. The shelves were still quaking, making more jars splatter on the concrete floor. But nothing else was moving. The rest of the basement was quiet. This wasn't an earthquake at all.

"What's going on?" he said aloud. None of this made any sense.

He reached out to grab one of the quivering shelves to make it stop, but his hand went right through it—as if the shelf were no longer there. A hole had appeared in the middle of the shelf, swallowing up the jars as it expanded. The hole, Xavier realized, went right through the thick concrete wall, so that the light from his phone shone into empty darkness beyond. A dim pinprick of red light appeared in the middle of the darkness, capturing his attention. It grew steadily larger, like the headlight of an oncoming train.

After a moment he could make out what it was.
The Crest.
The Crest of Ahoratos, glowing bright red, growing larger and more distinct against the curtain of black.
"Hurry, Prince Xavier," said a voice. Xavier knew instantly whose voice that was.
Still holding the seed, he jumped through the hole in the wall, running as fast as he could toward the light.

"Xavier?" Xavier's dad came down the basement steps and looked around. He was sure he'd heard glass breaking. Everything was quiet and intact. He walked over to the shelf of canned vegetables.

No Xavier.

One jar lay broken on the floor, its contents spilled out over the concrete. Xavier's dad frowned, puzzled. He bent down to pick up the glass pieces and noticed a footprint carved into the spilled tomato juice—a footprint with the grid pattern of a sneaker. And it was *facing* the shelf—as if Xavier had walked right into the shelf that lined the wall.

Xavier's dad stared at that footprint a long time. He wondered. Could it be?

As he picked up more shards of glass, the spilled juice on the floor began to move, as if an invisible finger was running through it. Xavier's dad held his breath as the drawing finally took shape, forming itself into the unmistakable Crest he'd known from long ago.

Xavier's dad knew then where his son had gone. He smiled to himself, cleaned up the mess, and picked out two more jars of tomatoes to take upstairs. He'd have to tell his wife that the boys might be late for dinner.

CHAPTER 13

Ahoratos Again

X avier?" said Brianna. "How'd you get here?"
Xavier spun around to find Brianna looking at him with a bewildered expression, as if he'd just dropped out of the sky. Maybe he had, he wasn't quite sure. Evan and Levi were staring at him too, although Manuel was too busy trying to keep his homemade shield from falling over.

Xavier remembered running into the shining Crest and feeling for a moment as though his own body had evaporated, melted away by the radiant red glow of it. "I was in the basement, getting tomatoes and . . . Oh, nevermind, I'm here now."

He was standing on the top of a tall hill overlooking what seemed to be the entire kingdom of Ahoratos. The bright sun shone from the golden sky above, bathing the scene in an ethereal radiance. He'd almost forgotten how beautiful Ahoratos could be when he wasn't dodging Ents or going over waterfalls.

"Tomatoes?" said Levi, raising an eyebrow.

Xavier waved his hand, brushing off Levi's teasing.

"Stellar," said Brianna. "We were afraid you'd get stuck back there or something."

"I see you got the shield to come through with you," Xavier said, turning to Manuel.

"Yes, as I suspected. I just had to be holding it," Manuel said proudly.

"Did you get your seed?" Brianna asked Xavier.

Xavier felt in his pocket. "Yeah, it's here. What about yours?"

"Got mine," said Brianna, pulling the box from her hoodie pocket and opening the lid. Like Xavier's, her seed was glowing faintly.

"Me too," said Levi, opening his hand to show them his seed.

"Where are we, anyway?" said Xavier. He turned in a circle to get the full view and caught sight of a tall mountain, the peak hidden in the clouds. Gazing at it, Xavier felt a surge of excitement run through his body. The mountain seemed to hold some sort of promise or challenge, beckoning to him.

"I don't remember seeing that mountain before," he said.

Levi looked to where Xavier pointed. "Me neither. Maybe it's new."

"A new mountain? Mountains are supposed to be old."

"Well, here in Ahoratos, you never know what's gonna pop up."

"There's Skot'os," said Brianna. They all fell silent, gazing at the far horizon, where the twisted metal spires of the Fortress of Chaós loomed up through a low-lying fog. Above the fortress loomed a giant sky-pod, bigger than all the rest of them put together. It was shaped like a flattened teardrop with a dark, lumpy underbelly.

"That skypod looks bigger than it did before," Xavier said. "Doesn't it?"

"Yeah, creepy," said Levi. "Shouldn't we find the Water and—"

"There it is!" said Brianna, pointing to the river below them that meandered between the lower hills. "I can see the Crest!"

The Crest hovered on the surface of the ambling river, shivering slightly.

"Well, that was easy," said Evan.

"Yeah, *too* easy, don't you think?" said Xavier, concern in his voice.

Evan puffed out his chest a bit. "Nah. We're just getting good at this stuff now, see? That Ponéros dude isn't going to mess with us anymore."

"Yeah, right," said Xavier, wincing at Evan's bravado.

"We should get down there," said Manuel. "I can't wait to show Ruwach my shield. . . ."

Suddenly Manuel's shield shuddered, nearly knocking him off his feet. The other kids jumped away in alarm.

"What was—?" Before Manuel could finish his sentence, he saw what had happened—they all did. Something was sticking out of his beautiful shield—the green metal shaft of an enormous arrow.

"Is that what I think it is?" said Evan nervously.

The kids glanced around, only to see another arrow descending out of the sky, headed right for them. They froze in horror.

"Attack!" Manuel shouted, cowering behind the shield. "We're being attacked!"

The second arrow, which was more like an Olympic javelin than a regular arrow, slammed into the ground near Evan's foot. Evan cried out and jumped behind the shield with Manuel. Soon the other three kids were cramming themselves behind the shield as more arrows fell all around them, coming so fast that the air seemed to sing with them. Another arrow thumped into the shield, the point piercing all the way through, just inches from Brianna's face. All the kids gasped in fright.

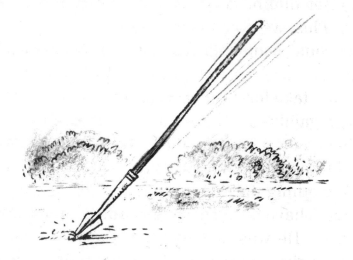

"Who's shooting at us?" Brianna cried, trying to steal a peek around the edge of the shield to get a look. "I can't see anyone shooting! Just arrows all over the place."

"Probably Ponéros, the 'dude' who doesn't want to mess with us," said Levi sarcastically, glancing at Evan.

"All the way from the Fortress?" said Evan, his voice choked with disbelief. "It's like a gajillion miles away."

"He must have long-range arrows," said Manuel. "*Ballistic* arrows."

"We need to get to the Water," Xavier said urgently. Another arrow slammed into the shield, making his ears ring. "Any ideas?"

"We could use the shield as a sled and slide down the hill really fast," Evan offered.

"That's a dumb idea," said Levi.

"It's not dumb," said Xavier. "But it won't be fast enough. Plus, we'd be too exposed."

"We could wait until they run out of arrows," said Levi.

"That'll take forever," cried Evan. "They've probably got like a gajillion. . . ."

"That's not a real number," said Brianna. Another arrow hit the shield, making them all wince. "We need to do something now!"

"Wait! I have an idea," said Manuel, calculating his next move. He was looking up at the sun, which was shining brightly overhead. "Everyone grab an edge of the shield." The others weren't sure what he was up to, but Manuel was already in motion.

"What are we doing?" Brianna yelled.

"I saw a movie once where an army used sunlight reflected off their shields to blind the enemy—"

"Was it a true story?" said Brianna, as they strained to hoist the shield into position above their heads.

"Doesn't matter," said Levi. "We're doomed if we stay here any longer."

Manuel nodded, pushing up his glasses. "Okay, so everyone grab an edge of the shield—we need to lean it back so it can catch the light—"

The kids worked together, pushing one side and pulling the other while Manuel kept peeking out, dodging arrows to see if the shield was positioned correctly. Finally, it tipped just right so that the entire shield seemed to be lit on fire with the reflection of the sun, almost as if it had become the sun itself.

"There!" Manuel shouted. "Hold it right there!" The kids held as still as possible. After a moment they could hear the barrage of arrows begin to lessen.

"I think the attack is slowing down," said Manuel.

"Then let's move!" said Levi.

"Right. We've got to do this fast, before they can take aim again. Ready?" Xavier looked at each of the others to make sure they understood. They each nodded. "Okay. On your mark. Get set—" He paused, listening. There was no sound of launching arrows now. "GO!"

The five kids picked up the shield and, still holding it aloft, made a run down the slope toward the Water. Soon arrows began to fly again, but not as accurately as before.

"Jump!" Xavier shouted as soon as they made it to the bank, which was so thick with mud that their feet sank. Brianna, Levi, and Evan quickly let go of the shield to slosh through the muck, throwing themselves into the Water as arrows fell all around them. Xavier noticed that the arrows didn't sink into the Water but bounced off as if they'd hit a solid wall.

"Come on!" Xavier shouted to Manuel. "We need to get in the Water—"

"But my shield!" Manuel cried, clinging to his shield even as he struggled to get his feet out of the mud. If Xavier let go, the shield would probably fall on top of Manuel and trap him.

"Okay," Xavier said. "I'll help you. But you need to move. Pull!"

Together they heaved the heavy shield through the thick muck, straining with all their might. Once Xavier was close enough to the Water's edge he shouted, "Jump! Now!" The two boys jumped, pulling the shield down over their heads; it disappeared below the surface of the Water just as the deadly point of a huge green arrow slammed into it.

CHAPTER 14

In the Cave

"That was close," said Evan.

The kids were safely in the Cave, wearing their warrior clothes and armor. Around them, Sparks flitted merrily.

"A little *too* close," said Levi.

"Good thing we had this shield," said Manuel proudly. "It probably saved us."

"I have a feeling that your shield is what helped the enemy find us in the first place," said Xavier. "You could see that thing for miles."

"You're just jealous because you didn't think of it," said Manuel.

"Oh brother." Brianna rolled her eyes.

"So you believe your shield will withstand any attack of the enemy here in Ahoratos?"

The kids whirled around to see Ruwach appearing from one of the tunnels. His voice was rather subdued. His long arms were tucked into his sleeves, so he looked smaller than usual. He approached the shield, examining it, his hood tilted slightly in curiosity.

"Well, sure," Manuel said a little more meekly. "I mean, it may look a little rough right now"—it had several large arrows still sticking out of it—"but it held up pretty well. This is only a prototype, of course. The next one will be even better. Titanium, maybe."

"Indeed," Ruwach said. "But the enemy you face has a knack for—changing tactics. And weapons. Are you sure you are ready for that?"

"Well, we'll be more ready with this shield than we will be with those seeds," Evan retorted. Xavier winced at his superior tone.

"I assume then that you did not bring your seed with you," Ruwach said.

"Uh . . . no," Evan said uncomfortably. "Figured I wouldn't need it."

"Is that why you threw it in the water of the pond instead of bringing it to the Water here in Ahoratos?"

Evan's mouth open and closed, shocked that Ru already knew what he had done.

"You said that thing was dangerous! It was making me nervous. I mean, I didn't want to get attacked *more* because I had a stupid seed in my dresser drawer."

"I have mine, see?" Brianna said proudly, showing Ruwach her lavishly decorated box. "Doesn't it look pretty?"

"Have you used it yet?" Ruwach responded.

"Used it?" Brianna wrinkled her nose. "How am I supposed to use it?"

"Ah, that is the point," said Ruwach. "If you had followed my instructions, you would know by now."

"We did follow the instructions," said Xavier. "We kept the seeds safe. Well, most of us anyway. See?"

Xavier opened his hand, showing Ruwach his seed. Levi did the same.

"Keeping it is not enough," Ruwach said. "The seed must be protected and used. As you will soon see, the enemy is on the move."

Ruwach moved to the center of the room—to the kids it seemed as though he hadn't moved at all, just disappeared from one place and reappeared in another. This was something they hadn't seen him do before. He raised his hand, and as the sleeve of his robe fell away, they saw the brightness of his palm as it glowed pure white. And then a beam of light shot out of it straight into the air, as it had once before.

"Look," Ruwach said. In the beam of light the kids could see the gnarled metal girders of the Fortress of Chaós. Something thick and black oozed from the many gaps in the girders; it took a moment for the kids to realize it was an army of Forgers spilling out of the fortress. From above, in the fortress towers, arrows continued to fly, soaring over mountains and valleys toward the golden land on the other side of the chasm.

"Forgers," Evan grumbled, staring at the image. "I really hate those guys."

"I'm not so crazy about them either," Levi added.

"Are they coming here?" Brianna asked.

"Are they coming for the key?" Xavier said. "The one we took? The one that opened the prison door?"

Ruwach withdrew his arm, and the vision vanished. "No, this time Ponéros is coming after *you*."

"Us?" said Brianna in a small voice. "All of us?"

"He knows if he can steal your seeds, he can weaken you. So he will attack. Quickly. And soon."

"So . . . what can we do to stop him?" Xavier asked.

"Show him you will stand. You will not back down."

"Just . . . stand?" said Levi, looking at the other kids in confusion.

"If we had swords, we could fight them." Evan spoke with a tinge of impatience. He really wanted a sword. "Wouldn't swords be a really good idea right about now?"

"You have everything you need," said Ruwach.

"Here we go again," said Evan under his breath.

"Can't we at least get whatever is in those locked rooms?" said Levi, stepping forward. "I mean, with just the five of us against a whole army—"

"You have everything you need," Ruwach said again.

"But these seeds . . ."

"The seed is your shield," said Ruwach. "Remember your instruction?"

The orbs on the kids' breastplates began to spin. Whenever the orbs awakened, the Warriors knew they would be given some sort of instruction that would help them on their quest. They waited anxiously as the words churned inside the orbs and then spilled out into the air before them:

If you have faith the size of the smallest seed, nothing will be impossible for you.

"Go now." One of Ruwach's long arms reached out, pointing to something behind the kids. They turned around to see what it was.

Nothing.

When they turned back. Ruwach was gone . . . and so was the Cave.

———

They were back on the hill where they had started. Skot'os still loomed, dark and ominous, on the horizon. But no arrows were headed toward them. It was quiet and peaceful. The sun shone brightly overhead, warming their faces.

Xavier looked down at the river, but there was no Crest rippling on the water anymore. He strained to see the lines of Forgers emerging from the gates of the Fortress of Chaós, as Ruwach had shown them in the vision. But he couldn't see anything through the fog.

An unseen enemy.

"Well, nothing's happening," said Evan. "How long do we just stand here?"

"Ruwach said to stand, so I guess we just have to—stand," said Brianna with a shrug. She held the seed in her hand, turning it this way and that and trying to figure out how to "use" it as Ruwach had instructed them to do. She really liked the way the jewels of the case sparkled in the sunshine.

Levi yawned. "Do you think sitting would be okay? I'm getting tired." He sat down on the soft grass. Brianna and Evan joined him. Manuel laid his shield on the ground and sat on top of it. He had to wedge himself between the arrows poking out of it, as he hadn't been able to pull them out. He closed his eyes and leaned his head against one of the arrows.

"Hey guys, don't fall asleep, okay?" Xavier remained standing. Someone had to be on the alert. On guard. He felt uneasy, although he usually felt uneasy in Ahoratos, particularly when it seemed peaceful. That was usually when everything went wrong. He seemed to be the only one who felt this way, however.

He looked around, examining the terrain. At the bottom of one side of the hill was the river. The other side sloped down to a thick grove of trees.

"Maybe we should go down there," Xavier said, pointing toward the trees. "It would give us more cover."

"I thought we were supposed to stay here and stand—or sit," Brianna said. She had started to pick tiny white flowers nestled in the grass and weave them together to make a crown.

"I'm with Xavier," said Levi. "It's getting kind of hot up here. We could use the shade."

"I don't want to carry my shield all the way down there," said Manuel, glancing down at the trees below. "I need to rest up a bit first."

"This doesn't seem like a very safe place," Xavier said. "Come on, I think we should go. We can all help carry the shield—"

Before he could finish, before any of them could begin to stand up and take a step toward the trees . . . a deafening roar rose up from the edge of the sky.

CHAPTER 15

The Olethron

W hat in the world is that?" Brianna screamed. She pointed toward the red sky over Skot'os, which had lit up like a supernova.

No one answered. They couldn't. Terror silenced them. The streak of light became bigger and bigger as it climbed into the sky. The kids soon realized it was actually a streak of *fire*. And it was headed straight for them.

"Run!" Xavier said. He turned and raced down the hill toward the trees. "This way! Hurry!" He stopped and turned to make sure the others were following, but they were still sitting on the ground, struggling to get up.

"I can't move!" Brianna said, pushing off the ground with her hands to no avail. It was like the ground was holding her down—she felt like she was stuck to it. "Help!"

Levi and Evan tried to get up as well, but they too were unable to release their limbs from the soft ground.

"It feels like it's pulling us down—" Levi said, grunting with the effort to free himself. Manuel, since he was sitting on the shield, had gotten to his feet, but he was struggling to lug the cumbersome shield with him down the hill with little success.

Xavier darted back up the hill. "Come on! Get up!"

"We can't!" Evan said.

"What's the matter?"

"I don't know—something's holding us down. . . ." Evan thrashed around some more.

"Take my hand!" Xavier ordered. Evan reached a hand up to Xavier, who grabbed hold and yanked several times before he was able to free Evan from the ground. "Okay, run!"

Evan started running for the trees as Xavier turned to Brianna. He used two hands to pull her up, although she felt twice as heavy as her small size. Then she and Xavier hauled Levi up from the ground after several tries.

"Now go! Hurry!" Xavier shouted, once they were all standing. He looked up at the giant fireball, which was rising to a high arc in the sky with a long tail of fire like a comet. But there was something else he noticed: the fireball had a face. Dark, blotchy eyes and a wide, gaping red mouth. The face of something so evil and monstrous it stilled Xavier's heart.

Evan, Brianna, and Levi scrambled down the hill toward the trees. Xavier turned to Manuel, who was still trying to drag his shield with him. He couldn't go three steps without stumbling.

"Leave it!" Xavier shouted. "Let it go! Just run!"

"No, no, I need it!" Manuel cried.

"Manuel, look!" Xavier pointed to the fireball now beginning its descent toward them. Manuel gasped and rose up, abandoning his shield, half-running and half-falling down the hill with Xavier.

"Take cover!" Xavier shouted as he skidded into the trees, crouching and pulling Manuel down with him. Brianna, Levi, and Evan also hunched over and covered their heads, just as an explosion ripped open the top of the hill. They could feel the intense heat and draft from the blast even where they cowered in the trees.

"Look at that!" Evan shouted, pointing to the hill, which now had a giant, smoking crater carved into one side.

"What was that?" Levi said. "A meteor?"

"It was the *Olethron.*"

All the kids turned to see Ruwach behind them. He hovered between two trees a foot off the ground, his body hazy, transparent, as if he were an apparition and not a real being.

"An . . . *Ole-thron*?" said Xavier. "A new weapon?"

Ruwach shook his hooded head slowly. "There is nothing new under the sun."

"My shield," said Manuel, in exaggerated anguish. "It's—gone."

"Any shield you make of your own hands cannot withstand the destructive power of the Olethron," Ruwach said. "But your seed can."

Another roar came from the sky. The kids gasped and dove for cover as another mighty Olethron burned its way through the air, sending up fountains of dirt and ash when it hit the ground. Xavier looked up to see what had happened and felt the intense heat scorch his face.

"We're gonna die!" moaned Manuel, his arms over his head.

"Get us out of here!" Brianna cried out to Ruwach, whose image was growing fainter in the thickening smoke from the explosions that wafted through the trees. Ruwach did not answer, just lifted up one long arm and pointed with his glowing finger . . . straight back toward the top of the hill from where they'd just come.

"What? We can't go up there! We'll be pulverized!" said Manuel.

Just then the kids' breastplates lit up, blinking rapidly. Xavier stood up slowly, turning until his breastplate stopped blinking and shone with a steady light. It, too, pointed to the hilltop, which was clearly under attack.

"No way!" said Evan.

"Hey, we've been through this before. We need to follow the Way of the Armor," Xavier said, determination in his voice. "Come on. Let's go."

None of the kids moved. They heard the thundering whine of another Olethron as it blazed through the sky. It landed more distantly, so they couldn't see the fire, but they felt the shudder of the ground under their boots. A moment later a shower of ash filtered through the trees, coating them like snow.

"Ouch!" Brianna said, wiping a bit of ash off her nose.

Xavier picked a piece of ash off his shoulder and looked at it, feeling the pulsing spark as it continued to burn. He felt his resolve waver. This weapon, the Olethron, was *real*. It burned with real fire. It meant total destruction.

Xavier saw the others staring at him, waiting for him to tell them what to do. Ruwach was no longer visible. Xavier paused, suddenly uncertain. He wondered if he might accidentally lead them into the path of the destroyer. But Ruwach, the breastplate—they'd never steered him wrong. Although they *had* steered him into what seemed like mortal danger more than once.

Xavier felt the seed warming in his pocket. He reached in and pulled it out. It was glowing again, as it had in the basement, but more brightly. Like a tiny red lightbulb.

The seed is your shield.

Ruwach's voice echoed in his ears. How could this tiny seed be a shield? He didn't understand that at all. But he knew from past experience that Ruwach couldn't possibly be lying, even when he was not telling them exactly everything.

Have faith.

The orb on his breastplate began churning different colors. Letters spilled out into the air, arraying themselves in the instruction they'd all received from The Book:

If you have faith the size of the smallest seed, nothing will be impossible for you.

Xavier's fingers closed over the seed. He held it tightly, feeling its warmth inch up his arm. Maybe just holding it would somehow protect him.

"I'm going," he said to the others.

"No, you can't!" said Evan. "You'll be in—*carcerated*!"

"I think he means incinerated," said Manuel.

"I'm coming too," said Brianna. She stood up and moved toward Xavier. She too held her seed tightly in her fist, still in its bejeweled case.

"Me too," said Levi hastily, once he saw that Brianna was going with Xavier. "I'm going too."

The three of them stood together, clutching their seeds. Around them more Olethrons exploded, making the trees, the ground, the very air shudder. Smoke burned their eyes. Evan and Manuel looked at each other.

"Not me," said Manuel. "I'm not going—without my shield."

Evan shook his head silently, looking at the ground.

"Fine then, stay here," said Xavier, although his heart fell at the thought of leaving his little brother behind. He glanced at Levi and Brianna. "Ready?"

Brianna nodded, holding her head high. Levi nodded with much less enthusiasm. Xavier turned and began walking resolutely out of the woods, toward the hill. Levi and Brianna followed, side by side. As they emerged from the woods, an Olethron rocketed toward them, filling their senses with noise and fire.

CHAPTER 16

Just Stand

Xavier, Levi, and Brianna stood stock-still until the smoke cleared. Xavier checked his face, his body, making sure they were still intact. The Olethron hadn't hit them, but the blinding flash and the awful noise had made him feel certain that it had.

"I'm scared," whispered Brianna. Xavier was too. But he didn't want the other two to see that. He looked up to the top of the hill, still smoking from the first Olethron attack. It seemed like a long way—far longer than it had been running down. Climbing that hill would be the hardest thing he ever did—harder even than walking into a sandstorm or navigating the Fortress of Chaós. But he knew, deep down in the pit of his soul, that he had to do it.

"You guys don't have to come," Xavier said, turning to Levi and Brianna. "Stay here with Evan and Manuel. It might be safer."

"We're coming," Levi said. He sounded braver than he looked. Brianna nodded in agreement, forcing her shoulders back, her chin lifted.

Xavier nodded and took a step forward. Immediately, another Olethron crashed down, this one only a few feet away, the blast knocking the Warriors sideways. For a long moment they were blinded by the smoke and falling ash, their hearing deafened by the concussive blast.

"Everyone okay?" Xavier said as the smoke cleared.

"Yeah." Brianna checked to make sure she still had all her fingers. "That was close."

Xavier was surprised to find that the three of them were still standing, despite the force of the explosion. Something about his boots felt different. He picked up one foot and noticed that steel hobnails had sprouted from the soles. The spikes had dug deeply into the ground, keeping the Warriors from falling.

"The boots!" he said. "Check it out."

Levi and Brianna both looked down at their feet, noticing the spikes in their boots for the first time.

"Stellar!" Brianna exclaimed.

"Yeah, cool," said Levi.

"They'll help us to get up the hill," said Xavier. With that he started and the others followed suit.

They had only taken a few more steps before another glowering Olethron came roaring toward them.

"The rock!" Xavier said, pointing to a large boulder partway up the slope. They scrambled to get behind it as the Olethron exploded just in front of them, most of the force of the blast absorbed by the rock, which shook and splintered as if it were made of glass. Brianna bent over, covering her head with her arms.

"I'm *really* scared now," she whispered.

"That makes two of us," said Levi.

"Three of us," said Xavier. "Come on. We need to move. Keep looking up. Don't look at those things. Remember crossing the Bridge of Tears? Stay focused, okay?"

Brianna nodded, wiping the tears and ash from her eyes. Levi, impulsively, grabbed her hand.

"I'm right here, Bean," he said. He smiled at her. She smiled back.

"There's a clump of bushes up ahead," Xavier said. "We're going to run to them and take cover again."

"I don't think we'll make it," said Brianna.

"We will. Our boots will get us there."

The three Warriors took off at a dead run for the clump of bushes, their boots giving them a firm footing on the increasingly treacherous terrain. They dove for the bushes just as another Olethron exploded, although this one was farther away. The brush did not give them protection, but it did give them a hiding place for the moment.

"Seems like they shoot when they can see us," said Xavier.

"Is there another place farther up to hide?" said Levi.

Xavier peeked around the brush to scout out the terrain. "I don't see one. We'll have to go all the way to the top from here."

"All the way?"

Xavier nodded. "I'll go first, you two stay behind me. Run as fast as you can. Don't stop."

"What if another Olethron comes?" said Levi.

Xavier glanced from one to the other, not knowing quite how to answer. He shrugged and said: "Duck."

"Duck?" Levi repeated. "That's it? Just duck?"

"It's all we got," said Xavier. Another Olethron thundered nearby. Brianna covered her ears, trying not to cry. Xavier looked at her. "You okay?"

She nodded, glancing at Levi. He gave her a reassuring smile.

"Let's do this," she said.

Xavier crouched like a track runner and took a deep breath. *On your mark, get set* . . . He heard an imaginary starting pistol in his head and took off for the top of the hill. *Just keep moving*, he told himself. *Don't stop.* He felt as though he could see a path laid out for him, perhaps projected by the breastplate, he wasn't quite sure. It did not go straight up but swerved this way and that, making the run take even longer. And yet he felt sure-footed, as if his boots were actually carrying him up the hill. The smoke stung his eyes and the blasts made his ears ring, but he could still run, still breathe. He felt energized, as if each step he took gave him the courage to take another.

He glanced back once or twice to make sure Levi and Brianna were following him. He shouted encouragements to them, straining to be heard over the constant roar of the Olethron.

"Almost there!" Xavier called out. An Olethron came crashing toward him. He shouted and dove out of the way, landing on his face, feeling rocks and dirt from the blast rain down on him. He raised his head—only a few more feet to go. He low-crawled the rest of the way, shouting for Levi and Brianna to follow his lead and stay low. He hoped they were near.

When finally he got to the top of the hill, he waited for the other two to join him. They crawled up on their bellies, coated in dirt and ash, hardly recognizable. They stayed still a moment, covering their ears in anticipation of another cacophony of noise.

It never came.

Levi cautiously removed his hands from his ears. He lifted his head and looked around.

"I think they stopped shooting," he whispered.

Xavier rose to his knees, poised in case the attack should start up again. He got slowly to his feet. Levi joined him. Brianna rose as well, gazing around in shock.

There was no beautiful view anymore. The world around them was ringed in smoke, patches of scarred and burned ground showing through here and there. The once grassy hill under their feet had been eviscerated, torn open, nothing but dirt and bare rock. Trees that were once fully in leaf had become crooked, blackened sticks. It looked like a war zone. Nothing moved but smoke and flame as far as he could see. Xavier felt nauseated as he thought of Evan. He wondered if his baby brother was okay.

"Did we do it?" Brianna said. "Is it . . . over?"

"I guess so," Xavier said in a soft voice, although even he couldn't quite believe it.

"Guess all we had to do was get to the top of the hill. That really wasn't bad at all," Levi said, a laugh bursting out of him that was really more of a gasp. "Well, it *was* kind of bad, I guess, but we survived, right? We should tell the other two it's safe to come out now."

Brianna turned back toward the grove of trees where Evan and Manuel were hiding. Nothing much was visible through the haze and flames. She hesitated, fearing the worst, and looked to Xavier in hopes that he'd call out to them. But his expression told her that he couldn't. So, she stepped forward, cupped her hands to her mouth, and shouted, her voice scratchy from all the smoke: "Hey guys! All clear!" She hoped the others couldn't tell how worried she was.

For a long, scary moment she saw nothing move at all. Then Evan and Manuel emerged cautiously from the smoke-rimmed trees and looked up at the three kids at the top of the hill. Brianna screeched with joy. Xavier let out a breath and bent over, closing his eyes in relief.

"Come on!" shouted Levi.

Evan and Manuel scrambled up to the top of the hill, skirting the large, smoking craters where the Olethrons had landed. As soon as they arrived, Manuel spotted blackened metal fragments that had been part of the shield he'd left on top of the hill.

"My shield!" he exclaimed. He bent over to pick up one of the mangled shards, but his sleeve caught on the sharpened edge. As he tugged it away he felt a stabbing pain. "Ow!" he gasped. He raised up his forearm to reveal a small gash that had already started to bleed.

"Oh, be careful!" Brianna said.

"It's destroyed." Manuel tossed the hunk of metal away and slumped in despair, nursing his wounded arm.

"Don't worry, Manuel, you were going to make another one anyway," said Evan, trying to make him feel better. "It will be even better, right?"

Manuel nodded mutely.

Evan turned to his brother. "No more Oreos?"

"*Olethrons*," said Xavier, trying to act as if none of it was any big deal.

"Awesome," said Evan. "So all you had to do was walk up to the top of the hill and the bad guys just went away? Guess we didn't need those seeds after all."

"Guess not," said Levi.

"So—what now?" Brianna asked. "Don't we go back to the Cave now?"

"Or to the castle, for some ice cream," said Levi, remembering the last time they'd successfully completed a mission. They were able to celebrate with a huge feast in the castle in the clouds.

"How do we get there?" Evan asked.

"Usually it just happens," said Brianna, glancing around. "Ru shows up, and then everything changes and we're just—there."

The kids waited a moment longer.

"Nothing's happening," said Levi.

"Wait," said Xavier, putting up a hand to stop their chatter. "Do you hear that?"

From somewhere far away there came a long, low rumble, like thunder gathering in the corner of the world. But it didn't come and go like thunder usually did. It kept on rumbling, growing louder. The smoke that lay over the landscape started to shiver, as if whatever was making the sound was sending shock waves through the air.

"Maybe the Forgers are coming now," Brianna said.

"We should go back down the hill," said Levi nervously. "Ru will probably be coming to get us. . . ."

"Look!" said Xavier.

They turned their eyes to the sky as the entire horizon seemed to burst into flame—a brilliant light shooting up from the veil of smoke, turning the red sky above Skot'os nearly white.

"What is it?" Brianna gasped.

"A nuclear bomb?" said Levi.

"I think it's the Olethrons," Xavier said softly. "Like—a *lot* of them."

The five kids inched closer together, frozen in fear, as hundreds of the huge flaming arrows—more like rockets, brighter than the sun—burst into the air and began to speed toward them, the ghoulish faces with gaping red mouths laughing at the Warriors' terror.

"There's too many—there's no escape this time," Levi muttered. The Olethrons filled their whole vision. They cowered low, shielding their eyes from the blinding light.

Xavier tried to think. What had Ruwach told them? *The seed is your shield.*

The seed. He'd almost forgotten about it. He opened his fist and looked down at the tiny seed. It glowed brightly, as if it were asking to be put to good use. It seemed to be burning with an energy deep inside itself. Xavier raised his gaze to the awful faces of the Olethrons advancing on them. Their progress seemed to have slowed, as if time itself was dragging its heels, prolonging this terrible moment. Giving him time. To think.

What sort of shield could stop these things? No shield ever made would be able to do that. So how could this little seed . . .

The seed is your shield.

If the seed was a shield, maybe he had to use it like one. Xavier's fingers closed around the seed, making a fist. Then he thrust his arm straight in front of him, just like he would with a real shield. As soon as he did, a sudden jolt shot down his arm. He thought for a moment that the Olethrons had already hit him, but then he realized something else was happening. Streams of infinitesimal red seeds, like electric sparks, burst out from between his tightly closed fingers, spewing out into the air around him. Xavier gasped, struggling to keep his arm steady as the streams of sparks formed a shell around him, a sparkling dome of tiny red lights that flared brightly against the white light of the approaching fireballs.

Something had definitely happened; Xavier knew that for sure. He wasn't imagining it. He was completely covered, enclosed in this ethereal, protective shelter that emanated from the seed in his fist. The air felt quieter suddenly, the roar of the approaching Olethrons muted. Xavier glanced at the others and saw them staring at him openmouthed. Even he wasn't positive of what had transpired, but he knew it was something amazing.

"What *is* that?" Brianna cried. Xavier could hear her, although her voice was muffled by the dome of seed-lights around him.

"Your seeds!" Xavier shouted. His voice sounded weird to him, like he was inside a tin can. He hoped they could hear him. He yelled even louder: "Raise up your seeds! Like this!"

Levi and Brianna immediately took out their seeds and followed his lead, raising their seeds in their fists. They too felt the jolt in their arms and saw their seeds open, shooting out fountains of tiny red seed-lights that covered them in a protective shell. They could still see the fireballs and hear the approaching whine of the Olethrons, but the sound seemed duller, less terrifying than it had a moment before.

"This must be the shield Ru was talking about!" Levi cried. Although it didn't look anything like a shield, nor did it look solid enough to stop the momentum of the Olethrons.

"I . . . I don't have one. . . ." said Evan in a shaking voice.

"Me neither!" Manuel said.

"Just stay close to us," said Xavier, pulling Evan to his side so that the two of them were covered by his dome. Levi did the same thing for Manuel. "Don't move. Just—stand!"

The kids stood frozen, watching the flaming rockets with the horrible faces plummet toward them. But as they watched, the faces of the Olethrons changed. They were no longer laughing. Instead, the empty eyes widened, and the mouths yawned open in what looked like fear. Horror.

The Warriors braced themselves for impact.

And in the next moment, the Olethrons crashed into them.

CHAPTER 17

Faith Like a Shield

No one dared to open their eyes. Except Levi.

And he almost didn't believe what he saw.

The screaming faces of the Olethrons seemed to have hit a wall, an invisible yet wholly impenetrable wall. The shield of tiny red seeds had repelled the flaming weapons as if they were no more dangerous than flickering birthday candles. When they hit, it seemed as though the whole world burst into flames.

But Levi felt nothing. The fire, the smoke, the ash, none of it touched him. He couldn't even smell anything burning.

"Look!" he shouted.

The kids watched as hundreds of massive fireballs ricocheted off their shield domes and sailed back toward the fortress, leaving trails of thick black smoke in their wake.

Levi saw that Xavier had his eyes open now too, his arm still tightly wrapped around his little brother. The Warriors watched, stunned, as the Olethrons converged on the jagged girders of the Fortress of Chaós. For a moment there was complete silence. And then a great fire rose up from the entire horizon, obliterating the fortress from view and engulfing the giant skypod above it in a belching cloud of black smoke. Several deep booms resounded before the fire dispersed, leaving nothing but empty, smoking ruin.

And just like that, it was over.

"Is that for real?" said Brianna, hiding her eyes with one hand while still holding the seed out before her.

"Gotta be," said Levi. "The fortress is like . . . *smoked*!"

"I don't mean *that*. I'm talking about *this*!" She gazed around herself at the protective shield that had repelled the Olethrons and kept them secure.

"It's real all right." Xavier lowered his fist; as he did, the sparkling seed-lights of the dome retracted. Levi's and Brianna's did the same thing. When they opened their hands, they saw that the seeds no longer glowed—they looked like ordinary red Skittles again.

Before their eyes, the huge craters nearby that had been created by the Olethrons began to close up and disappear. The blackened trees regained their green leaves, the grass regrew, filling in the black holes. Ahoratos looked as it had the first time they had come to this hilltop. All signs of the enemy were gone, except for that giant skypod that still floated in the red sky, above where the Fortress of Chaós had stood only moments before.

"Awesome," said Levi, smiling for the first time.

"Way awesome," said Xavier.

"The seed is your shield," said Brianna, repeating Ruwach's words. "I get it now. Stellar." She pulled out her little case and put her seed carefully inside. A few of the jewels came unstuck from the lid and fell off. She picked them up to stick them back on but then changed her mind and stuffed the case and the jewels in her hoodie instead. She didn't really need it after all.

"So that's what my mother meant about the seed having power—I never would have thought a tiny seed could do that." Manuel scratched his head. "I tested the seed. . . . It couldn't have . . ." He stopped, then hung his head sadly. He wished he'd never flushed that seed down the toilet.

The group wasn't surprised when the world around them began to spin.

"Hang on everyone. I think we're leaving!" Xavier said, pulling the others together in a huddle. It felt like a ride at an amusement park, the kind that spins around and around so the riders are plastered to the edge by centrifugal force. But it was over nearly as quickly as it began, and the kids found themselves back in the Garden of Red, surrounded by all the weird plants and vines, which leaned in toward them as if still terribly interested in the seeds they carried.

Ruwach greeted them, spreading his long arms in welcome. "Well done, Warriors!" he said in a nearly jovial voice. "I see you have learned how to use your shields."

"Why didn't you tell us they did that?" Levi asked.

"But I did," said Ruwach with a small shrug. "I told you the seed was your shield. You just had to believe that. To *use* it like a shield."

"Stellar," Brianna said. "But Xavier actually figured it out."

Xavier blushed as they all looked at him. But then he noticed that his brother and Manuel had taken a few steps away from the group, their shoulders slumped. They stared at the ground, as if they were ashamed. Xavier turned back to Ruwach.

"Could you possibly give them—another one?" he asked in a low voice.

"Yeah, you must have more buried in the dirt here," said Brianna.

Ruwach shook his hooded head. "Each Warrior is given only one. But it can never be lost."

Evan looked at Ruwach forlornly. "But I threw it in the pond!"

"I flushed mine down the toilet," said Manuel in a miserable voice.

"Manuel, you are a fine young scientist," Ruwach said. "There is much you can learn from your experiments. But there is much more you cannot."

"Yeah, I guess so," Manuel answered.

"Let us go back to the Cave. We will talk more there."

Ruwach turned and sped down the path as the portal to the Cave once again opened for him. The others followed close behind—all but Brianna. A movement caught her eye—something flashing silver, which seemed out of place in this garden. She turned to see what it was and gasped when the flashing thing flew right at her. At first she thought it was an Ent and was about to try and swat it away. But when it lighted on one of the vines, she saw it wasn't an Ent at all. Ents usually started out looking like large, colorful butterflies, but then their wings would turn to sharp-edged metal as they revealed their long, black stingers. But this creature didn't look like a butterfly at all; it was small, silvery, and had eight thin, delicate wings, more like blades, almost transparent. It was magically beautiful, like nothing Brianna had ever seen before. She approached it cautiously.

"Don't fly away," she whispered to the creature. "What are you, anyway?"

She got so close she could look into the silvery thing's eyes. They weren't red, like the Ents. The eyes of this creature were clear blue, like tiny pools of water. Brianna was thoroughly delighted.

She reached out a hand toward the creature, which stepped nimbly onto her finger on slender silver legs. Its eight wings fluttered and flashed brilliantly. It was a rare and wonderful jewel that Brianna was sure no one else had ever seen before.

It settled on Brianna's finger, folding its wings as if completely content there. And right then Brianna knew she had to keep it. She was certain that a creature this beautiful and unique couldn't be dangerous. And since it came from the same place as the seed, which she was allowed to take back to earth, she couldn't imagine there'd be any reason why she couldn't take this creature as well.

She smiled. This little thing, whatever it was, would be all hers. Something no one, not her friends, and especially not her sisters, would ever have.

"I'll call you—Stella," Brianna whispered. "It means 'star.'" For this creature looked like a tiny, twinkling star. "Here, ride in my pocket. I'll keep you safe." She drew her hand slowly down toward her pocket. Stella didn't fly away. Even when it went all the way into the pocket. It was as if it wanted to go home with her.

"Our little secret," Brianna said as she headed for the portal back to the Cave. "Don't make a sound!"

The creature stayed very quiet.

Evan lagged behind the rest of the kids as they followed Ruwach back through the Corridor of Keys. Ruwach was still talking, telling them more about the wonders of the shield and affirming them for their courage. The guide lauded how well they had been able to destroy the mighty Olethron and the Fortress of Chaós in Skot'os.

Evan didn't think it was wonderful. He felt miserable. He'd thrown away his shield.

Then he remembered the key.

He stopped in the middle of the Corridor of Keys and looked around quickly until he found it—the plain wooden box he'd seen before. He darted over to it and opened the lid. There was that peculiar key with the four crosspieces, lying on the purple satin lining. The key to the rooms! The locked rooms that Ruwach still hadn't shown them. He felt certain that this had to be the right one. He reached out and carefully picked it up. He lifted it closer to his eyes, wondering if maybe there were more seeds in those rooms. Or other weapons that would be just as useful. He'd just borrow the key, go check out his room, and then replace it before anyone knew it was missing. That sounded like a great plan.

Just then he heard footsteps behind him.

"Evan!" It was Brianna, coming in from the garden. "Thank goodness—I thought I went the wrong way. . . ."

Startled, Evan slammed down the lid and shoved the key in his pocket.

"No problem," he said, raising an arm to indicate she should follow. "It's this way."

"What are you doing?" Brianna asked, glancing at the box he had just closed.

"Nothing . . . just looking at stuff. Come on." Evan hurried in the direction the others had gone.

Brianna took one more look at the box Evan had been hovering over, curiosity overtaking her. "Hey, isn't that the box—"

"You coming or what?" Evan called out irritably. Brianna shrugged and followed after him.

They traveled down several dark passages, unsure of exactly where they were going. The tunnel wound around in several directions, and for a moment Evan thought they were completely lost. By some miracle they turned a corner and found themselves back in the central den of the Cave. Ruwach was standing before The Book, with Levi, Xavier, and Manuel gathered around him.

"Hey, I just waited for Brianna," Evan said, blustering a little as he joined them. "I didn't want her to get lost."

"I wasn't lost," said Brianna. "I was just admiring . . . the plants in the garden. Sorry I took so long." She shrugged, smiling nervously.

Ruwach nodded, his hood turning from one to the other very slowly, as if he were studying the two of them intently with his invisible eyes, seeing into their very souls. Evan and Brianna both squirmed a bit under this silent perusal, their hands thrust into their pockets— each one for a different reason. Then Ruwach tipped his head forward, so that none of the kids could see the dark space where his face might be. He remained that way a long moment before raising the hood again and pointing to The Book. Evan and Brianna both let out silent breaths of relief.

Evan glanced around quickly, looking for a place he could stash the key. But then The Book opened, the pages flipping, emitting a multitude of low hums. The kids gathered around to watch. The flipping slowed then stopped altogether, and the scrambled letters lifted from the page, rearranging into place above their heads:

Let your faith be like a shield,

and you will be able to stop all

the flaming arrows of the enemy.

"Here in Ahoratos," Ruwach added, "and on earth." There it was again—the mention of a battle on earth. Xavier opened his mouth to ask a question, but before he could utter a single word, Ru gathered the floating words together and flung them into each of the orbs in the kids' breastplates.

"Awesome," said Levi. "We got this. No more Olethron for us."

"Yeah, stellar," said Brianna brightly.

Evan and Manuel said nothing. Xavier, noticing his brother's disappointment, turned to him and held out his seed.

"Hey, Van, my seed is your seed. Capeesh?"

Evan just shrugged. He might not have his seed, but he did have the key. He was sure if he could get away for a moment he'd be able to open his locked room and get something even better. Then he'd put it right back.

"Yeah, me too," said Levi to Manuel. "Just stick with us; we'll take care of you."

"What if—you're not there," Manuel said. "What if I'm alone and something happens—"

"You have everything you need," Ruwach said. "Always."

"Um . . . is there a bathroom in this place, by any chance? 'Cause I kind of need one," Evan said aloud. He hopped from one foot to the other in order to make his point. Ruwach's hood swung in his direction.

"Are you kidding?" said Xavier, flicking him on the back of his head. "You can wait till we get home."

"No, I can't—"

"Yes, you can! Look, it's time to go anyway." Xavier pointed toward one wall of the Cave, which was starting to fade away. Ruwach had disappeared. The other kids had started moving toward the disappearing wall. "Come on, Evan!" Xavier grabbed him by the sleeve, but Evan resisted, looking around frantically. *There!* A small indent in the bottom of one of the stalagmites, like a mouse hole. He could hide the key there. Evan started toward it. But Xavier caught him by the back of his collar. "Now, Evan!"

Evan held tight to the key in his pocket as his brother dragged him toward the disappearing wall.

CHAPTER 18

Found

Evan sat on the bus and stared despondently out the window. He had the whole seat to himself. Even that annoying kid Charlie had found someplace else to sit. The sky outside was dark and gray. It looked an awful lot like the sky over Skot'os after the Olethron attack.

He didn't like to think about that. It reminded him of how he had tossed away that seed, his shield, because he hadn't believed it could really protect him. When he had returned from Ahoratos, the first thing he did was run out to the pond to see if the seed had somehow washed up on shore. Ruwach had said it couldn't be lost, right? He had hoped that time would have reversed, like it sometimes did when they came back from Ahoratos, so that he could get a "do-over" and start again. He would know better this time.

But the seed never turned up. It wasn't on the banks of the pond or floating on the surface of the water. Nor was it anywhere in his room or in the bedside-table drawer. He had actually cleaned his entire room looking for it. His mother had been pretty happy about that. But no seed appeared.

He'd been so sad about losing the seed that he decided not to go to the Rec for a while. He couldn't stand being around his friends, who had their seeds and were all proud of themselves for having faith in what Ruwach had told them. He wondered if Manuel was with them today or if he had gone straight home too.

Evan got off the bus and went straight to the mailbox. There were a bunch of catalogs and a bill from the electric company. Nothing for him. He sighed, folding the mail and tucking it under his arm. He turned to head down the driveway to his house but then stopped and glanced up at Manuel's window, across the street. He saw Manuel there, looking out at him. Manuel didn't seem to be doing any experiments. He was just staring out the window. Evan waved. Manuel waved back. He looked as forlorn as Evan felt.

Evan thought about going over to Manuel's house, maybe just hanging out, checking out some of the crazy stuff Manuel had in his room. But he changed his mind—he didn't think he'd be very good company. He wondered if Manuel had been looking for his seed too. But Manuel had flushed his down the toilet—no way that thing was ever coming back again.

As Evan turned back to the driveway he caught sight of something, a sliver of red, in the tall grass at the base of the mailbox. He furrowed his eyebrows, wondering what it was. Probably one of those annoying sales flyers Mom was always complaining about. It must have gotten loose and fallen into the grass. That happened all the time. He almost walked away from it but then changed his mind and decided to pick it up.

He reached down, parting the grass, and picked up the red object. It wasn't a flyer; it was a small red envelope with no stamp or return address. It looked as though it had been there for a while, because the paper was all puffed and wavy, like it had been out in the rain. But it hadn't rained in over a week. Thank goodness Mom's tall grass had trapped it, otherwise it probably would have blown away.

Evan stared at the envelope in amazement. There in fancy, old-fashioned handwriting, was his name. The envelope was addressed to *him*.

And Manuel.

The mail in Evan's hands slipped from under his arm and dropped onto the ground. He stood staring at the envelope. His heart raced with some unnamed hope. He looked up at Manuel's window.

"Hey!" Evan shouted. "Manuel!" He began jumping and waving his arms wildly, shouting the name over and over, so that Manuel had to open his window to see what Evan was so excited about.

"What's the matter?" Manuel called back.

"Come look at this!" Evan shouted.

"What is it?"

"A letter! For you! For us!"

"Wha—?"

"Come here! Right now!"

Manuel's head disappeared from the window. A moment later his front door opened, and he came bounding out, just as Evan went charging up his driveway, still waving the envelope in the air.

He showed Manuel his name on the front of the envelope. "Did you open it?" Manuel asked, breathless from his short sprint.

"Not yet."

"Well, do it!"

Evan hesitated, then tore it open. He looked inside expecting to see a card or at least a piece of paper folded into a handwritten note. Instead it looked like nothing. Just a hollow envelope of . . . red.

But there was something—some things—tucked into the corner. Two small red objects that dropped out onto his hand when he tilted the envelope over.

"Whoa!" Evan said softly.

Manuel peered down at the seeds in Evan's hands. Something like a bubble puckered in his gut at the sight of them, actually at the sight of *one* of them. He picked it up and examined it closely. A tear stung the corner of his eye. "This one is mine," he said almost too quietly for Evan to hear. "See the scratches? I made those when I was experimenting on it."

Evan leaned in, his eyes widening at the sight of the scratches. Then, he remembered that he'd bitten his seed to see how hard it was. He lifted the one in his hand close to his nose for a better view. There were teeth marks—*his* teeth marks—indented on the sides. "This one is definitely mine. It still has the teeth marks from when I tried to bite it."

Both boys were quiet for a moment as they tried to make sense of it.

"How did they get in that envelope?" Evan wondered aloud.

"Ru must have put them there."

"But this envelope has been here awhile. Since it rained. Before we even went to Ahoratos and got the seeds in the first place. So how—"

Evan and Manuel both fell silent again. Sheer amazement gripped them as they tried to process how their very own seeds could have been in this envelope *before* they had even received them from Ruwach. *Before* they had thrown one in the pond and flushed the other one down the toilet.

"Well, since it isn't possible," Manuel said finally, "it must be Ruwach."

"Yeah," Evan said softly. "Whoa."

"He said we couldn't lose them, remember?"

"Yeah, I do," said Evan. "Guess he wasn't kidding, was he?"

Manuel laughed. "I don't think he ever kids."

Evan held the seed up between two fingers. He glanced beyond it, into the sky. "You think he's watching us, right now?"

Both Manuel and Evan looked up into the sky, searching for Ruwach's familiar form in the clouds.

"I don't see him," said Manuel. "But I think he is."

"Yeah," Evan said with a laugh. "He always is." He felt a drop of rain on his nose and looked up again. More drops fell on his face. Thunder sounded distantly. "Looks like rain," he said.

Evan and Manuel said good-bye to each other, racing back to their own houses, eager to put their seeds in a safe place. The rain fell harder, stirring up a mist in the road that took on the shape of a small figure in a flowing robe, long arms stretched out toward each of the children as they went on their way.

PART TWO

Head Spinners

CHAPTER 19

Stella

*B*rianna sits alone on the bench outside the rec center, watching the activity around her. On one side the basketball game is in full swing. Xavier and Evan are playing with a bunch of other kids. Mr. J. Ar is the ref, as usual. Ivy stands on the sidelines, watching. Xavier passes by—he pauses to glance at Ivy. She smiles. Her red hair shines in the sun. Xavier smiles back. Brianna frowns. Why is he smiling at her? Does he think she's pretty?

Brianna looks over at the skateboard park, where Levi is skating with his friends. She wants to go over and talk to him. There is something important she has to tell him. But she just can't seem to move from the bench.

Rook walks across the field, a large chainsaw slung over his shoulder, a thick tree limb under his arm. He glances at Brianna and smiles in greeting. She looks away without returning his smile. She hears a noise and turns back to see Rook standing there, the tree limb at his feet. He's dropped it. He is staring at the ground. She follows his gaze, wondering what he is looking at.

Right in the middle of the pavement a crack appears, a hole that begins to get wider and wider.

Brianna feels the ground under her feet rumble. The inside of the hole comes alive, breaking into thousands of tiny shards that rise up, filling the air, making a horrible noise. Brianna stands, suddenly realizing what those flying things are: Ents. A huge swarm of Ents, the savage metal butterflies from Skot'os. They are here now. On earth. Coming. For them.

The kids on the playground are soon engulfed in Ents—the kids on the basketball court, those at the skate park, the jump ropers, the volleyball players, the girls sitting in circles in the grass, taking selfies and texting them to each other. Yet they don't seem to notice. Clouds of Ents spin in circles around the kids, a spiral of black metal wings and blazing red eyes.

Brianna gets up from the bench and walks solemnly toward the Ent swarm. Rook tries to grab her, pull her toward the rec center. She wrenches away from him. She is not afraid. But she doesn't know why.

"Brianna!"

Someone is calling her. Mr. J. Ar perhaps. Or her grandfather, Grandpa Tony. It kind of sounds like Grandpa Tony. What is he doing here? How did he know there was going to be an Ent attack? That doesn't make any sense.

"Bean!" Levi yells at her. He comes toward her through the cloud of Ents, holding something in his hand, something round and glowing white. She can't figure out what it is. She shakes her head and turns away from him to run in the direction of the invading Ents.

"Bean! Come back!"

Brianna looks up at the Ents coming for her, raising her arms. They begin to clutch at her with their iron claws, pulling her up, into the air, so that she is flying with them—

"Wake up, Breeny!"

Brianna opened her eyes to see her sister Crystal shaking her shoulders and scowling at her. She sat up, her heart racing. She was flying with the Ents—about to be carried away. And then she wasn't.

"You were making that whimpering-babbling noise again," Crystal said, yawning.

Brianna looked around the room—the rumpled beds crammed together, the mounds of clothes piled up everywhere, posters of their favorite boy bands lining the walls. Her three sisters glaring morosely at her through their tousled hair. Outside the window the sky was red—was this Skot'os? No. It was just the dawn. The normal, earthly dawn. Brianna didn't know whether to be relieved or disappointed.

"Sorry," she said.

"Never mind," said Crystal, flopping back on her bed. "Still got twenty minutes before I have to get up." She closed her eyes. The other two lay back down as well, pulling pillows over their heads.

Brianna got up and went to the window. She gazed out at the sunrise, waiting for her heart to stop thumping. She'd been having the same nightmare for the past several nights. An Ent attack on the rec center. She hadn't told anyone about it, not even Levi. It was just a dream, after all. And it wasn't all bad, at least she didn't think so. The flying part—that was sort of fun. Even if she was being carried away by evil Ents, there had been something sort of thrilling about that part.

She heard a soft buzz in her ear and turned to see a sparkle of light flitting about her head.

"Stella!" she whispered, holding her finger out for the pretty little bug to sit upon. "Did I wake you up too?"

Your sisters should be more understanding. Stella batted her eight wings—they flared slightly, pulsing with an inner light.

"I know," Brianna said, nodding. "They think because I'm younger I don't count for anything."

You should show them.

"Yes, I should. Show them." How would she do that? Brianna wasn't sure. She'd have to think of something.

She'd managed to keep Stella a secret since returning from Ahoratos with the tiny creature tucked in her hoodie pocket. It hadn't been hard—Stella always managed to disappear whenever anyone else was around. But when Brianna was alone, Stella would come out and play happily, fluttering around her room or riding on her shoulder. Brianna often thought the creature was speaking to her, although she never actually heard a voice out loud. She could just tell what Stella was thinking. Sometimes Brianna even responded out loud—once Crystal had happened by the room and poked her head in, looking at Brianna with concern.

"Who are you talking to?"

"No one, just learning lines from a play we're doing in school," Brianna had answered. The lie came out so easily; she hadn't even had to think about it.

"You're weird," Crystal had announced before walking away.

Brianna didn't even have to speak to Stella, for the beautiful little creature seemed to know her moods. When she was sad, Stella was sad. When she was mad, Stella was mad, her little inner lights flaring and pulsing. When Brianna was happy, Stella buzzed around the room doing silly dances of light. Stella was wonderful.

Brianna still wasn't quite sure what kind of butterfly Stella was, or if she was a butterfly at all. There was nothing that matched her in the encyclopedia or in any of the online searches Brianna had done. The closest was a rare insect called a *jewelwing damselfly*—it was such a pretty name that Brianna wished she had made it up herself. Except the damselfly had only four wings, whereas Stella had eight beautiful, blade-like wings, so delicate and glittery. She could be some other, even rarer species of the damselfly, one that no one had even discovered yet. Brianna was thrilled to think that she was the only one in the entire world who knew about it.

Why don't you skip school today? Tell Nana Lily you are sick so you can stay home and hang out with me. Stella seemed to whisper into Brianna's ear without making any sound at all.

"I could pretend to be sick," Brianna whispered aloud. "I could stay home. No one would miss me at school." Levi preferred hanging out with his skater friends at school. And Xavier was older—he wasn't in any of her classes. Plus, he was obsessed with making the basketball team these days; he never had time to talk to her anymore. And then there was Ivy—that girl with the nice hair. Ivy was in a bunch of her classes, and she was very smart.

Whenever she was called on, she always knew the right answer. Brianna was getting pretty sick of it.

Besides, she hadn't done her math homework. Usually she got her homework done as soon as she got to the Rec so she'd have the rest of the time to hang out with her friends. But lately, she'd been putting it off. Sometimes she didn't do it at all. It was like she just didn't care anymore. She didn't know why. Middle school was so different from elementary school. At first it had been exciting and even challenging, but now it just seemed long and boring.

She knew her grandfather had noticed a change in her. He'd look at her over the dinner table with his head cocked sideways, like he was trying to figure her out. Every once in a while he'd ask her what was wrong. She wanted to tell him, but she just didn't know what to say. That was weird too—Brianna never used to have trouble saying what was on her mind. Now she hardly talked to anyone. Except Stella.

Yes! Stay home! Pretend to be sick!

But then Nana Lily would make her stay in her room all day. "If you are sick, you'll need to rest," she'd say. Or she would take her temperature and look down her throat and insist there was nothing wrong with her. She'd know Brianna was faking being sick and would make her go to school anyway.

So Brianna got up and, trying to be as quiet as possible so as not to wake her sisters again, began to get dressed. She went into the bathroom to brush her teeth and put on a fresh layer of glittery lip gloss. She tried to comb her hair, to make it lie flatter and smoother, but it wasn't cooperating this morning. It rarely ever did.

Ivy has such pretty red hair. So shiny and straight.

Stella wiggled on top of Brianna's unruly curls. Brianna frowned. She forced an extra wide headband on the top of her head, to hold her hair down. Stella flapped out of the way, then burrowed under the mass of Brianna's hair, right at the base of her neck. She flattened her transparent wings against Brianna's skin, her glow fading until she was nearly invisible against Brianna's golden-brown complexion.

Outside the bathroom window a large butterfly lit upon a tree branch. If Brianna had turned to look, she would have seen it. And if she had seen it, she would have known what it was, even though its large, metallic wings were folded up. There was no mistaking this creature. It was an Ent. Stella, fixed to the back of Brianna's neck, parted the thick hair with two of her wings and turned her cold, blue eyes to the huge Ent. The Ent's red eyes flared, flashing, sending Stella a message, like Morse code.

Is she ready yet?

A little more time, Stella replied, pulsing back the message. *But not long. I promise.*

CHAPTER 20

Out of Sorts

Brianna sat at the breakfast table, stabbing at her oatmeal with her spoon. She wasn't feeling hungry. The dream replayed over and over in her mind. And her sisters were really annoying her. Crystal was complaining to Nana Lily about Brianna's making all that noise and waking them up nearly every night this week.

"It's bad enough I have to listen to Nikki snore," Crystal said.

"I don't snore," said Nikki, making a huffy face.

"*You* sing in your sleep," Winter said to Crystal.

"Even if I do, there's a difference between singing and snoring," Crystal retorted. "I can't get any sleep in this house!"

"I should have my own room anyway," said Winter. "I'm the oldest."

"Breeny can't help it if she has bad dreams," said Nana Lily kindly. "Part of growing up."

"I need my beauty sleep!" Crystal huffed.

"You sure do," said Brianna under her breath.

"What was that, Shrimp?" Crystal glared at her.

"Nothing."

Good one. Brianna brushed the hair off the back of her neck, feeling a slight tickle. She smiled to herself. That *was* a good one.

She looked up at the wall. A calendar hung there by an old-fashioned wall phone with a long, curly cord. Who had phones like that anymore? No one she knew. Just her grandparents. The calendar had a date circled in red. Brianna's birthday. Friday. She'd almost forgotten about her birthday. Beside the calendar was a framed needlepoint sign Nana Lily had made years ago: *Fix your thoughts on what is true, and honorable, and right, and pure, and lovely. . . .*

Brianna looked back down at her oatmeal. *This oatmeal sure isn't lovely.* She wished they could have something else sometimes. Like pancakes or waffles. But Nana Lily only bought cereal or oatmeal.

"You going to help me clean up the attic after school?" Grandpa Tony said, eyeing Brianna thoughtfully. "There's something I'd like to show you."

Brianna shrugged. "I don't know."

Why do you always have to help him? How come your sisters never have to do anything?

Brianna scratched the back of her neck again. Her neck had been itching a lot lately—maybe she got a bug bite in her sleep. She looked at her grandfather. "Why do I always have to help? Why can't Crissie do it? Or Winny? Or Nikki?"

Grandpa Tony's eyes got big. He glanced at his wife, who looked worriedly at her coffee cup. "I thought you liked helping me."

She paused for a moment. She did enjoy it. Well, at least she used to. "Well, I don't. It's boring." Brianna got up and left the table. She didn't even take her dishes to the sink.

———

"What's the matter, love bug? You seem out of sorts these days." Nana Lily smoothed the back of Brianna's hair while she put on her sparkly sneakers at the front door.

Brianna shrugged. "Nothing. Just tired." She stood up to put on her jacket. Outside, colored leaves blew against the window in a stiff breeze.

"Not getting enough sleep? Because of bad dreams?"

"Maybe."

"Are you sure that's all?" Nana Lily gazed upon her youngest granddaughter, worry lining her face. She knew Brianna was still sad about her mother abandoning them, even though she had been pretty young when it happened. Brianna had never even met her own father. She used to ask where her parents were and when they were coming to get her, questions Nana Lily never had a good answer for. And now Brianna was getting to the age when everything got harder for a girl. Her older sisters had gone through the same thing, although they had adjusted pretty well. But for Brianna, it was different.

Brianna glanced up at her grandmother's gentle face. She shrugged. "I don't know."

"You'll tell me if you do know, won't you?"

"Guess so."

"Hey! I know someone who has a birthday coming up," Nana Lily said with a twinkle in her eye. "You're going to be twelve years old very soon! I have a special surprise for you."

"What is it?" Brianna asked. She hoped it would be a hoverboard. She'd seen one in a magazine with a pink and purple swirly design. She'd mentioned it to Nana Lily once or twice, dropping hints whenever she could.

She's not going to buy you a hoverboard. You never get anything new.

"If I told you, it wouldn't be a surprise!" said Nana Lily. "You'll just have to wait and see, won't you? Have a good day at school today, okay? Give your old nana a hug." Nana Lily opened her arms, and Brianna fell into them, hugging her tight.

Brianna jumped down from the top step of the porch to the sidewalk like she always did and began skipping toward the bus stop at the corner.

Don't skip. You look silly doing that.

She stopped skipping, even though she usually loved to skip, and walked more slowly, glancing around to make sure no one had seen her. She reached up to check that her headband was still in place and patted her hair to try to make it lay down flatter.

Too bad you don't have hair like Ivy.

Brianna scratched her neck.

When Brianna got on the bus, she saw Ivy sitting by herself. Ivy smiled at her. Her ruby hair looked shinier than usual. Brianna almost smiled back, until she caught sight of Ivy's cool, hip backpack. She wished then that she had asked Nana Lily for a new backpack for her birthday.

You never get anything new.

Brianna averted her eyes and walked hurriedly past Ivy, tossing her chin in the air as she did. Then she sat next to a younger kid at the back of the bus.

There. Bet that girl feels bad now. The voice wasn't scolding; it sounded pleased. Brianna smiled to herself. *I hope so.* She pulled her lip gloss out of her hoodie pocket and applied a fresh layer, smacking her lips in satisfaction.

CHAPTER 21

The Key Keeper

Evan rode the bus to the Rec, looking out the window at the yellow and orange leaves blowing across the road. He knew there'd be big piles of leaves at the rec center. Rook had a big leaf-sucking machine that he rode around the property. But instead of bagging the leaves up right away, Rook would dump them in a huge pile for the kids to jump in. He was cool that way. Even Mr. J. Ar had taken a liking to him.

The bus slowed as it turned into the rec center loop. Evan stuck his hand in his pants pocket, just to be sure it was still there. The key. The one he'd taken from the Cave. He hadn't meant to take it. He was hoping they'd go back to the Cave soon so he could put it back before anyone noticed it was missing. It made him a bit nervous to keep it in his pocket all day, but he couldn't take a chance on leaving it somewhere where his brother, or his mom or dad, might find it. His mom especially; after all, she did have eyes in the back of her head.

It had been so hard keeping the key a secret. Evan was kind of surprised that Ruwach hadn't come looking for it. Maybe he didn't even know it was missing. He never seemed to use it anyway. Maybe Ruwach just made up all that stuff about not being able to take anything back to earth from Ahoratos—because so far, nothing bad had happened to Evan because of it.

Besides, he didn't mean any harm. He just wanted to take a peek in his room—the locked chamber beside his suit of armor in the Cave—just to see what it was that was so valuable and powerful that the enemy wanted to make sure the Prince Warriors never got it. Then he would put the key back right where he found it. No one would ever know the difference.

Evan also checked to make sure his seed was securely in his backpack. He still wasn't sure why Ruwach insisted the kids bring their seeds with them to earth, since they left all the rest of their armor back in the Cave. But Ruwach probably had a good reason.

It had been two weeks since their last journey to Ahoratos and their victory over the Olethron. Since then they had gotten some messages from the app, but the glowing Crest had not appeared to any of them. Evan wondered why they hadn't been called back—maybe Ponéros had really given up his attacks. After all, the Olethron apparently destroyed the Fortress of Cháos. Maybe Ponéros was busy building himself a new fortress and didn't have time to start another war with the Prince Warriors. That sort of made sense.

Evan got off the bus and crossed the parking lot to the rec center. He went inside to see if the other kids had arrived yet. He saw Brianna, sitting by herself at a table, a book in her hand that she wasn't actually reading. She'd been doing that a lot lately. She was getting—moody. Evan had heard that girls tended to do that when they got into middle school. He thought it best to steer clear of her.

"Hey, Evan." Mr. J. Ar came out of his office, a whistle around his neck. "Going to shoot some hoops today?"

"Nah. . . . It's leaf-vacuuming day," Evan said, looking out the window.

"Oh, yes, better get out there before the pile is gone. Bit windy today."

"Yeah . . . hey, Mr. J. Ar, what's with her?" Evan pointed to Brianna.

Mr. J. Ar sighed. "I'm not sure. I'll go talk to her. You go on outside."

Evan watched Mr. J. Ar go and sit by Brianna then shrugged and sped out the back door to see the gigantic pile of leaves Rook had created in the middle of the playground. Already a dozen kids were demolishing it. Evan looked around for Xavier and spotted him over at the skate park with Levi, practicing kick flips. Xavier was getting pretty good at them. Rook sat on his leaf-sucking machine, drinking from a bottle of water while Manuel showed him a yellow leaf, probably explaining why it was yellow.

"Hey," Evan said, going over to them. Rook turned and smiled at him.

"Hey, Squirt."

"Evan! I was just telling Rook about why leaves change color in the autumn. I'm doing a project for science class."

"It's pretty cool," Rook said with a grin.

"Nice pile," Evan said, pointing to the leaves.

"Yeah. Biggest one yet."

"I need to collect more specimens for my project. Do you want to help me, Evan?" Manuel asked.

"No, thanks," Evan replied. Like he would ever.

"Okey dokey. See you later!" Manuel trudged off to find more leaves.

"Better get in there before it's pulverized," Rook said.

Evan looked at the pile. He wanted to join in, but there was something else on his mind.

"Hey, Rook, you . . . been back lately?"

Rook nodded nonchalantly. "Sure."

"Really? When?"

"All the time."

Evan was stunned and a little jealous. "Really? How come you get to go and we don't?"

"I don't really know the answer to that."

"So how do you get there if you aren't called? Mr. J. Ar said there was a way, but he wouldn't tell us how."

Rook looked uncertain. "Well, I think you'll figure that out, when the time comes."

"You sound like Ru now," said Evan with a sigh.

Rook laughed. "Be cool, Squirt. You'll get back there. . Just be patient."

Evan shrugged, as if he wasn't quite sure he believed Rook's words.

"So . . . what's going on . . . over there? Any more attacks from . . . you know who?" Evan lowered his voice and leaned in so only Rook would hear him. "Ponéros?"

Rook's eyes narrowed; he spoke in a conspiratorial whisper. "Not that I know of. But there *is* a problem."

"What's that?"

"The key is missing again."

Evan froze. "The key? What key?"

"The key to the rooms. The locked rooms."

Evan tried to look surprised and confused. "You mean the key you stole in the first place? I thought Ruwach got that back."

"He did. But it's gone again." Rook looked levelly at Evan. "It wasn't Ponéros this time, or any of the Forgers. Who do you suppose would do that? I mean, anyone who knew what happened to me would certainly never do such a thing, would they?"

Evan felt his own face grow hot. "Yeah, I mean no. No way. That would be . . . dumb."

"That's what I thought," Rook said. "Ruwach wants me to find it, get it back."

"Yeah? So—you been looking?"

"Yep. No luck so far. Any ideas?"

Evan looked away. For a moment he wondered if Rook already knew and was giving him a chance to come clean. "Maybe—one of the prisoners you brought back from Skot'os? Like one of them could have been— what do you call it? A mole, that's what it is. A mole."

Rook nodded slowly. "Yeah, maybe. Might have to look into that. But I'm hoping whoever took it will just put it back."

"Yeah . . . I bet that's what they'll do," Evan said in a smaller voice.

"Because if that key ended up in the wrong hands, it could mean disaster all over again."

Evan glanced over nervously, but Rook's gaze was fixed on the kids jumping into the leaf pile. Evan stuck his hand in his pocket to make sure the key was still there. "That would be bad, I guess," he murmured.

"Very bad."

Ivy walked into the rec center; it was nearly deserted except for Mr. J. Ar, who was sitting at a table talking to Brianna. Brianna looked sad, sort of dejected. Ivy wondered why. It wasn't like her. Brianna was usually always busy, always involved in something. Either she had a project to work on or she would be out playing basketball or watching a game, cheering on her friends. Maybe there was something wrong at home. Ivy wanted to talk to Brianna a dozen times; it was part of Ivy's assignment, and a difficult one for a girl usually overcome with shyness. She wasn't sure why Ruwach wanted her to do this—to make friends with a girl who obviously didn't want to be friends. She'd assumed that Ruwach wanted her to teach Brianna something or help her somehow. But this was hard. Brianna was going out of her way to avoid her. *Why doesn't she like me?* Ivy wondered.

She went to sit at a table alone and took out her homework. It was hard to concentrate. Maybe she should go outside while it was still nice. She'd like to skate over at the skate park, but there were too many kids there already. She didn't like skating in front of other people. She practiced a lot at home, and she could even do a few tricks. But here it was different.

Wish I could go back to Ahoratos, Ivy thought as she pulled a geography book out of her backpack. *I'm not so afraid of things there as I am here*. She thought of the last time she was in Ahoratos, helping Rook get out of the fortress in one piece with his metallized prisoner. She'd felt courageous and confident. That had been fun. Slightly scary, but still fun. She hadn't heard from Ruwach since then.

She glanced over at Mr. J. Ar and Brianna again. Mr. J. Ar was talking softly, but Brianna didn't seem to be responding at all. Like she wasn't even listening—

Mary Stanton suddenly appeared in the office door, the phone crooked on her shoulder. She looked worried, as usual.

"Mr. Arthur, urgent call!"

Mr. J. Ar got up and went to take the phone from Mary, who hovered nearby nervously. Brianna hadn't looked up. *I should go over and talk to her,* Ivy thought. *She looks like she could use a friend.* Ivy rose, gathering her courage. *Now or never.* She took a step toward Brianna, but Mr. J. Ar interrupted.

"Brianna! I need to take you home immediately." Mr. J. Ar burst through the office door and hurried toward Brianna, his urgency mounting with every step.

Brianna looked up, her brows knitted together. "What for?"

"It's your grandmother. There's been an accident."

CHAPTER 22

Leaves and Leaving

Brianna saw the flashing lights of the ambulance as soon as Mr. J. Ar turned down her street. She felt as though she couldn't breathe at all, like all the air had been sucked out of the car. The ambulance was parked on the curb, along with a police car. A group of neighbors had come out of their homes to see what was going on.

Mr. J. Ar pulled up to the house as two men rolled a stretcher out the front door and into the open back of the ambulance. Grandpa Tony followed, looking as pale and shocked as Brianna had ever seen him. Her three sisters stayed on the porch, shaken and scared.

Brianna jumped out of the car as soon as it stopped and ran to the stretcher that held her grandmother. But it was already being loaded into the ambulance, so Brianna couldn't see Nana Lily at all.

"Grandpa!" she cried, running to her grandfather. "What happened! Why are they taking her away?"

"She just collapsed. . . . I don't know. . . ." He shook his head, holding back tears. "Brianna! Wait!"

Brianna didn't wait. She broke away from her grandfather and plowed past her sisters into the house. She ran up the stairs to her room, slamming the door behind her. She threw herself on her bed and began to sob.

Ruwach must not love you very much if he let this happen to your grandmother.

The voice was soft and insistent. Brianna opened her eyes to see Stella fluttering before her face, her delicate wings catching the light from the window.

"You're right," she said. "Nana Lily was the only one who loved me. There's no one who loves me now. I'm all alone."

That must make you very sad—and angry.

"Yes, I am angry." Brianna felt a heat building up inside of her. Outside, a siren whined. She went to the window to see the ambulance pulling away. Brianna's sisters stood in the driveway with their arms around each other, sobbing. Grandpa Tony must have gone in the ambulance too.

Brianna shut the curtains. She went down to the kitchen. There was flour all over the floor, a plastic tub of sugar tipped over on the counter. Nana Lily must have been baking a cake when she fell. A birthday cake. For Brianna.

Brianna looked up at the framed needlepoint on the wall: *Fix your thoughts on what is true. . . .* She walked over, took the frame off the wall, and threw it in the wastebasket. She collapsed at the kitchen table, her head pressed to her folded arms, sobbing.

You're not alone, Brianna. I'm here.

The voice echoed in Brianna's ear as Stella settled once more onto the back of her neck, her transparent wings disappearing against Brianna's skin.

I won't leave you like Ruwach and the Source did. Or like your parents did. I'll always be with you.

"At least I have you," Brianna whispered. "I'll never go back to Ahoratos again."

The large, metal Ent fluttered outside the kitchen window, its red eyes pulsing a message. Stella blinked back a reply:

Almost there.

———

"What's the matter?" said Levi. He'd stopped skating as soon as he saw his father coming out to the skate park. Mr. J. Ar had a very stern look on his face, as if something had gone terribly wrong. Levi picked up his board and went to meet his father at the edge of the park. Xavier, seeing the two of them, followed along.

"Brianna's grandmother fell—they think she might have had a stroke; she's been taken to the hospital. I just came back from driving Brianna home."

"Is she okay?" Levi asked.

"Don't know yet. I think we should all go over there and see if we can help. I just came back to get you. Xavier, if you and your brother want to come too, just let your parents know—"

"Look!" It was Manuel who spoke. He'd been nearby picking up leaves, but now he was staring at the pile Rook had created, pointing.

Levi, Xavier, and Mr. J. Ar turned to look. The leaves on the top of the pile were spinning in a circle, as if they were caught in a strong breeze. But then they lifted off the pile, swirling themselves into—*something*. A definite shape that rose steadily above the leaf pile. Evan and Rook, still by the leaf-sucking machine, saw it too. But no one else on the playground seemed to realize what was happening.

"What's it doing?" said Levi.

"It looks like—" Xavier began.

"It's the Crest."

They turned to see who had spoken—Ivy stood behind them. She could see it too.

"It can't be," Levi said. "It's just leaves—"

"I think she's right," said Xavier. Just then his phone buzzed in his pocket. He took it out and looked at it. The Crest glowed on the screen. He showed it to the others. Levi and Manuel both checked their phones— the Crest was on their screens as well.

"We need to go," Xavier said.

"But what about Bean?" said Levi. "We can't just leave her—"

"I'll keep an eye on her until you get back," said Mr. J. Ar, turning to head back to the rec center. "You kids better get going. Ruwach must have an assignment for you."

Xavier dropped his skateboard and began walking toward the leaf pile. Levi and Manuel followed. They joined Evan and Rook, who were standing by the leaf-sucking machine, still gazing in amazement at the swirling red and gold leaves, which had definitely formed into the Crest of Ahoratos.

"Hey, guys, all done now," Rook said to the kids still playing in the leaf pile, oblivious to what was really going on. "I need to get this pile bagged up before it gets any windier." The kids groaned a bit but moved away, finding other things to occupy themselves. The Prince Warriors gathered around the leaf pile, looking from one to the other.

"What do we do?" Levi asked.

"Jump in," Rook said.

"In the leaves?"

"Sure. Why not?"

"On three," said Xavier. "One, two—"

"Wait!" Manuel cried. "I need to get out my inhaler, there's probably a lot of dust in that pile—"

"Three!"

All four boys leaped as high as they could, jumping feetfirst into the pile. A storm of leaves rose up around them, as if sucking them down within its depths. They disappeared from view, and the leaves settled back down, an ordinary pile of leaves once more.

Rook waited a moment, just to make sure the kids were really gone. Then he aimed his leaf-sucking nozzle at the pile in order to gather up the leaves. He stopped when he saw the girl with the red hair walking toward the pile, her eyes fixed on the Crest. Rook smiled.

"What are you waiting for?" he said.

"Really? I should go too?"

"You see the Crest, don't you?"

She nodded.

"Well, better get moving then."

Ivy nodded and took a running leap into the pile, just as the floating Crest disintegrated into red and gold leaves that fluttered lazily to the ground.

Rook smiled to himself and turned on his machine again. He sucked up all the leaves into a giant bag then closed it up and hauled it away.

CHAPTER 23

Swirling Sand

T his is new."

Evan was the first to speak, standing up to brush the leaves off his pant legs. The others did the same, gazing in awe at the strange new surroundings. Even for Ahoratos, this was extremely weird.

They appeared to be at the bottom of a very narrow canyon. But the walls didn't go straight up. Instead, they swirled around in striated colors—reds, purples, pinks, oranges—as if they'd been stirred with a giant paint stick. A single shaft of golden light beamed down through the narrow slit of the canyon, illuminating the brilliant colors.

"How do you get out of here?" said Manuel, looking around, concern on his face. In fact, the wondrously carved walls appeared to surround them completely. He touched one purple formation, and it crumbled under his fingers. "It's sand!" he exclaimed. "Solid sand. Like sandstone, except as soon as you touch it, it disintegrates. This is fascinating! It's like a sand castle. . . ."

"Well, don't touch it anymore!" said Levi. "We don't want the walls to collapse on us."

The boys instinctively put their hands in their pockets.

"This reminds me of sand art we used to do in kindergarten," Evan said. "Remember? You pour in different colored sand—"

"Yeah, I remember," said Xavier.

"The leaves are gone," Manuel said. He pointed to the ground, where several small piles of colored sand appeared where the leaves they'd brushed off their clothes had been a moment before.

"They turned to sand too," said Levi.

"I don't see any water," said Xavier, looking around.

"Makes sense—any kind of water would probably collapse this place," said Manuel, rubbing his chin.

"Maybe we got dumped in the wrong place," said Evan.

Before anyone could respond, there was a loud *thump!* and a cascade of leaves fell down on them. Followed by something else. A person.

A girl.

"Hi," she said brightly, brushing leaves out of her glossy red hair. The leaves, like the rest, fell to the ground, making small piles of sand. "I'm Ivy."

"Oh yeah, I know you," said Levi, in a somewhat unfriendly voice.

"What are you doing here?" said Evan, clearly annoyed. "We didn't invite you."

"You didn't, but Ruwach did." Ivy's courage had returned. Ahoratos did that to her. She tossed a lock of hair out of her face defiantly. "He called me, same as you."

The boys looked at each other, dumbfounded. Was this that mousy girl who never talked? To them, she'd always just been a wallflower. How would she ever have enough backbone to stand up against Ponéros and his attacks?

"You've . . . been here before?" Xavier asked.

Ivy shrugged, nonchalant. "Yeah, a few times."

Xavier and Levi exchanged looks. Levi crossed his arms over his chest.

"Well, then, if you've been here before, you must know where the Water is," Levi said, folding his arms over his chest. "Since you know so much—"

Xavier nudged him. "Be cool, man," he whispered.

Ivy smiled, as if she weren't insulted at all. "Well, I can't say I've been to this exact spot before, but I have been in the Sand Canyon once or twice—"

"Sand Canyon?" said Evan.

"Yeah, it's pretty cool, isn't it? Except for the sand grobel . . ." Her voice trailed off, and she looked around. "Like I said, this particular place is sort of new to me, but if I had to guess I would say . . . the Water is through there."

She pointed. The boys turned around to see a narrow area of dark purple running between two of the canyon's swirling walls. It had looked solid at first, but on second glance, they realized it was actually an opening.

"How come she saw it and we didn't?" Levi muttered to Xavier.

"You have to know what to look for," Ivy said matter-of-factly. "This place can be tricky. Lots of optical illusions. The enemy is always trying to trick us. We need to go in. But you should be careful—if you bump into one of these sand walls, the whole thing could come down on your head."

"Is it safe?" asked Manuel, craning his neck to peer into the crevice.

"Who said anything about safe?" said Ivy with a laugh.

Manuel folded his arms. "I would not recommend going in there."

"Me neither," said Evan, also folding his arms.

"Suit yourself." Ivy turned sideways and shimmied through the narrow space, disappearing into the purple dark beyond.

The boys stood still, looking at one another.

"Did that just happen?" said Evan.

"You were kind of tough on her," Xavier said to Levi.

"She doesn't belong here. We're here to help Bean. . . ."

"How do you know we're here to help her?" said Xavier.

"Because . . . she's in trouble. Her grandmother is sick, and she's . . . well, she isn't here with us, is she? So she must be in trouble. And this girl doesn't have anything to do with that."

"How do you know?" Xavier asked. "If Ru called her here, maybe she does. Besides, she obviously knows what she's doing. She's trying to help us."

"Yeah, I'm with Xavier. We should go in after her." Evan turned to his big brother. "You first."

Xavier sighed and walked toward the crevice. It was so dark he couldn't see anything beyond it. Nor was the Crest anywhere in sight. He glanced back at the others once more then turned sideways as Ivy had, careful not to touch the walls of the canyon as he slid through.

Xavier heard a sound like water dripping from a spout. The air around him felt damp. Slipping through the narrow gap, he was immediately engulfed in darkness, unable to see ahead of him or behind him. He took a tentative step in the same direction, hoping there wasn't a wall there. His best course of action was just to keep going straight, in hopes that the path would be clear.

With another step, he noticed a tiny speck of light in front of him. The speck soon became a crack, getting taller and taller as Xavier continued to move toward it. Soon, he slipped through the opening and found himself in an open area, standing at the edge of a still pool. He breathed a sigh of relief that he had made it through. The water of the pool was multicolored, reflecting the brightly colored sand walls around it. The Crest hovered on the surface. This was definitely the Water.

He paused to gaze around at the amazingly beautiful sand formations. Then it dawned on him that the sound he heard was not from dripping water, it was dripping sand. The sand walls all around the Water were melting away very quickly, like a sand castle at high tide. Soon, the entire cavern he stood in would collapse.

Xavier turned to tell the others he had found the Water and to come as fast as they could, but he could no longer see the way he'd come through. Apparently, it was a one-way trip. He called out, "Levi! Manuel! Evan! Hurry! This whole place is going to implode!" But there was no answer. His voice echoed through the canyon walls, making the sand shiver, cascading down in little avalanches. *Better not make too much noise,* he thought. It was clear his friends couldn't hear him.

He looked into the Water. Ivy must have already gone in—he saw no sign of her anywhere. She could have waited for him. He wondered if he should wait for the others or figure out some way to communicate with them. But the walls were melting even faster now. Like one of those timers made of sand, and once the sand ran out—

No time to think about it now. He had to move. He couldn't go back, and he couldn't wait. He shut his eyes and jumped into the Water. . . .

The next thing he knew he was standing next to Ivy in the Cave. He blinked, thankful that the familiar glowing stalagmites and stalactites looked solid, unmeltable. Sparks danced around his head in greeting. Ruwach was nowhere to be seen.

"Your friends coming?" Ivy asked.

"They're on their way. I hope. You should have told me the whole place was about to melt."

"I didn't know," said Ivy. "It's always different. Don't worry, they'll be here. They've come through the Water before, right? They'll be fine."

Xavier couldn't help but worry, even though there was nothing he could do about it. He wished he had this little girl's confidence. He noticed that she was dressed like he was, in the dark gray warrior clothes with boots, belt, and breastplate already on, although hers, like Brianna's, held a faintly iridescent sheen.

"This is new," Ivy said, pointing to the center of the room, where a large, old-fashioned steamer trunk sat, the kind people used to take on long voyages in the olden days. It was made of a dark, rich wood with brass rivets all around the edges. The domed lid was held in place with a large brass lock plate.

"What's it for?" he asked.

"Don't know."

"Did you try to open it?"

"Yup. But it's locked."

Xavier glanced at her. "So—how many times have you been here?"

"A few," said Ivy with a shrug.

"Just on your own?"

"Sometimes."

"Do you know how many . . . *others* there are?"

"Oh, lots," said Ivy. "Why? Did you think you were the only Prince Warriors?"

"No, it's just that—I never saw you here before. With us, I mean."

"Yeah, I think maybe it has to do with your friend Brianna. I've noticed that she's been acting—different—lately. Although I'm not sure what I can do to help—I think she sort of hates me."

"Why would you think that?"

Ivy shrugged. "She avoids me." She paused, wondering whether or not she was saying too much. "Ruwach wants me to make friends with her. So far I've done a pretty bad job, I guess. I've tried to be friendly, but she just walks by as if I don't even exist. Sometimes I catch her looking at me, but as soon as I do, she looks away."

"Why does Ruwach want you to be friends with her?"

Ivy shrugged. "He didn't tell me that. Of course."

"Well, he must have had a good reason. Ru doesn't do anything without a good reason." Xavier thought about this. "Maybe he just wants her to have a friend. I mean, a friend that's a girl." She never did seem to hang out with other girls. Although lately, she hadn't been hanging out with anybody. She'd been acting pretty weird. But Xavier had just thought it was one of those girl things. Now he began to wonder if it were something more serious.

Just then there was a noise like a heavy curtain being ripped down the middle, and the other three boys arrived, looking slightly bewildered but unhurt.

"'Bout time you showed up," said Xavier under his breath, although he was actually relieved to see them.

"You could have told us," Evan said with a scowl. "We almost got trapped in that place!"

"But you didn't," said Ivy with a smirk.

"That's true. We are getting better at this," said Manuel, pleased with himself. "But the sand formations were fascinating, wish I could have stayed longer— "

"Where's Ru?" said Evan, interrupting.

"Beats me," said Xavier.

"Bet she knows," said Levi sarcastically, pointing to Ivy. "She seems to know everything."

"Hey, I just got here too," Ivy protested.

"Warriors." The voice thundered through the Cave, making the stalactites shiver and bringing the kids' conversation to an abrupt halt. Ruwach appeared at the entrance of one of the many tunnels that ringed the room. But he wasn't alone. Someone stood beside him. A teenager just a little older than they were, with a dark complexion and deep-set eyes. His expression was guarded, as if he were unsure of these kids who had just arrived.

"Finn!" Ivy exclaimed, running toward him. "Remember me? It's Ivy!"

Finn's face softened in recognition.

"Oh . . . yeah. You're the girl who helped me get out of the fortress."

"She did what?" said Levi incredulously.

"I was just helping Rook out of a jam and ended up helping Finn too," Ivy said. She turned to Finn. "You look tons better than the last time I saw you."

Finn just smiled, a little embarrassed. The rest of the kids looked at each other in shock.

"How did she . . . ?" Levi began.

"Finn was a prisoner of Skot'os," Ruwach announced, his deep voice commanding everyone's attention. "He was rescued by Rook. I have melted his metal parts and broken his chains. He's been here learning the ways of the Prince Warriors. He asked to meet you."

"Why did he want to meet us?" said Xavier.

"To thank you." It was Finn himself who spoke. "You rescued Rook, and he rescued me. Without you, I would not be free. I am deeply in your debt, Prince Warriors." He bowed a little. "And you, Princess," he said to Ivy.

"Aw, it was no big deal," said Ivy with a wave of her hand. Levi rolled his eyes.

"Your courage has been commendable," Ruwach interjected. "But you will need even more courage for what is coming next."

The word *next* hung in the air over the Warriors' heads, heavy and ominous.

Levi took a step toward Ruwach, his face clouded with worry. "Is this about Bean? Is she okay? My dad told us—"

Levi couldn't finish because Ruwach cut him off. And his next words would change everything.

"A portal has been opened."

CHAPTER 24

The Sypher

The kids stared at Ruwach, not understanding.

"What portal? And why?" Levi asked.

"Someone brought something back to earth, something I had not allowed." Ruwach's words were punctuated with an underlying anguish that the children had not heard before.

Evan felt his heart beat faster. He thrust his hand into his pocket—the key was still there. He needed to put it back as soon as possible. But then he would never get to see inside his locked room.

Xavier looked around at the others. "Not any of *us*," he responded confidently. "We haven't taken anything, except for the seeds."

"Something very . . . dangerous." Ruwach's voice reverberated through the Cave. His hood scanned all their faces.

The kids looked at each other, suddenly fearful. Evan pulled his hand out of his pocket and put both hands behind his back. He glanced about, trying to act as innocent as possible, but he could barely breathe.

"Maybe it was her," said Levi, pointing to Ivy.

"It was not me," said Ivy, her face reddening at the accusation. "Maybe it was you."

"I didn't take anything!"

Levi and Ivy began to argue.

"Come on, you two, cut it out!" Xavier said. He glanced at Ruwach, who stood motionless, his hands folded into his long sleeves. Something about his stance gave Xavier the shivers. This was clearly more serious than he thought. Levi and Ivy seemed to notice it as well and fell silent. All the kids began looking at each other, wondering which one of them had taken something from Ahoratos.

Evan shifted his gaze to the floor, fear gnawing at his belly. *He's got to know it's me,* he thought. He opened his mouth to confess about the key, but Ruwach suddenly spoke aloud.

"Where is Brianna?"

Levi and Xavier exchanged looks.

"We figured you didn't call her," Xavier said.

"She wasn't at the Rec with us. Her grandmother had to go to the hospital," Levi said. He paused, thinking of something new. "Wait a minute . . . was *she* the one who took something?"

Ruwach did not answer.

"But she wouldn't do that!" Levi protested. "She would never—" he stopped, falling silent again.

"What was it?" said Xavier softly.

"I think I know."

The kids spun around at this new voice to see Mr. J. Ar, in full armor, standing behind them.

"Dad!" Levi said. "What are you doing here? I thought you were going to take care of Bean—"

"She wouldn't listen to me. I had tried talking to her before we got the call about her grandmother, but she would barely say two words in a row. I got to thinking about that—this change in her. That's why I'm here. I began to wonder if Brianna might have been infected by a . . . Sypher."

"A Sypher? What's that?" said Levi.

"It's like an Ent," began Mr. J. Ar, "but more specialized, more subtle. Syphers attach themselves to someone and have the ability to twist and contaminate that person's thoughts. That's their goal. Ponéros sends them for that purpose."

"You mean like the jedi mind trick? Cool," said Evan.

"Not exactly like that. They cannot control a person's thoughts, but they can make suggestions that are very tempting and attractive. To the point where a person may not be able to distinguish their true thoughts and feelings from those of the Sypher." Mr. J. Ar looked at the Warriors. "Was there a time when Brianna was alone here? Where she might have come across one?"

Evan spoke up. "She stayed in the garden after we all left—I saw her in the Corner of Keys—"

"Corridor," corrected Xavier under his breath.

"Why didn't you tell us before?" Levi turned to Evan, his voice accusing.

"I didn't even know she did anything!" Evan said. "I thought she was just . . . you know . . . dawdling. She does that a lot. Especially when there's flowers and stuff around."

Levi looked at Ruwach. "Did you know she'd taken something?" Ruwach was silent. "Why didn't you stop her?"

"I cannot stop anyone from making wrong choices. I can only help them make the right ones." There was deep sadness in Ruwach's tone, rooted in love, as if he would have done anything to prevent Brianna from suffering the consequences of her choice.

Evan bit his lip, his hand going back into his pocket again. He *had* to get the key back in its box as soon as possible. He looked around for the little mouse hole he had seen the last time. It was so far away. He wouldn't be able to go over there without everyone noticing. His gaze moved to the various tunnels that encircled the Cave—one of them led to the Hall of Armor, where those locked rooms were kept. But which one? They all looked the same. This Cave was way too confusing.

"So if this thing has attached itself to her," Manuel was saying, "why can't we just go over to her house and . . . unattach it?"

"It is not so easy," said Ruwach solemnly. "Once the Sypher has locked on, only the person infected can get rid of it. And quite often, the person does not want to because her thoughts have been so distorted by the Sypher. You will have to convince Brianna that she must rid herself of it."

"But you said something about a portal opening. What does that have to do with the Sypher?" asked Levi.

"If something from here is brought to earth without permission, it opens a portal between the seen and unseen worlds," Ruwach explained. "Which will allow more of its kind to come through."

"More—Cyclops?" asked Evan in a small voice.

"Syphers," said Xavier, bopping him on the head.

"So that's how it works," said Manuel. "One Sypher will open the portal for more Syphers?"

"Not only Syphers," said Mr. J. Ar. "But Ents as well. Think of the Syphers as Special Forces, designed to infiltrate a place and make a clear path for an invasion."

"An invasion?" asked Levi slowly. "What kind of invasion?"

"An invasion of the Unseen," said Ruwach.

"So you're saying—there's going to be an invasion? On earth? Soon?" Xavier asked.

"Very soon," said Ruwach.

"And what can these Syphers or Ents or whatever they are do to us? Can they—kill us?" said Evan in a tiny voice.

"Syphers do not kill physically," said Ruwach. "But they will take over the mind so that you cannot think clearly, and worst of all, you are no longer able to hear my voice and receive clear instruction from the Source. The Ents do the same thing with their darts. The dart itself can wound, but it is the poison in the dart that causes the most damage—it hardens the mind as well as the body. So all a person can hear are the lies of the enemy rather than the truth of the Source."

There was silence, the kids pondering what this could mean.

"We need to close that portal," said Xavier finally.

"And capture any entity that comes through the portal—Ent or Sypher or any other slave of the enemy," added Mr. J. Ar.

"How do we do that?" Xavier asked.

"Might I suggest some really potent bug spray—" Manuel began.

"First," Ruwach interrupted, "you will need the protection of the helmet."

He spread one arm to the trunk. The latch unbuckled itself, and the lid creaked open slowly, releasing a wide beam of white light. Six round, hazy objects floated up from inside the trunk and hovered in the air. At first they looked like white balloons, but as they grew more distinct, the kids could see they were transparent helmets. Smooth and round with extra coverings for the ears and neck.

"Cool!" said Evan, excited.

"They'll protect us from the Syphers?" Xavier asked.

"From any enemy force that seeks to control your mind," said Ruwach.

"They look like bike helmets," Levi muttered, unimpressed. "They're gonna make us look like dorks."

"Some of us *are* dorks," said Manuel. Evan laughed. Levi rolled his eyes.

"If you go into this coming battle without your helmet, you will become something much worse than that," said Mr. J. Ar, looking at his son reprovingly.

"Sorry," said Levi, hanging his head.

"James," said Ruwach, "give the Warriors their helmets."

Mr. J. Ar nodded and moved toward the hovering helmets. He reached out to pick one. When his hands touched it, it became a solid object, no longer transparent. He handed it to Levi, who put it on his head. As soon as he did, the smooth, plastic-looking surface seemed to break into facets, each tiny flat surface reflecting and magnifying the dim light of the Cave.

Even the Sparks grew interested, clustering around the helmet for a better look.

"Whoa," whispered Evan. "It's like a . . . a . . ."

"Geodesic dome," Manuel finished for him.

"What's that?"

"It's kind of like a—circle, built on a network of intersecting circles," Manuel said, not very helpfully. "It makes the whole structure stronger."

"With this helmet, you can withstand all the attacks to your mind that the enemy can throw at you," Mr. J. Ar said. "As long as it's on your head, of course."

"I can't feel it at all," said Levi. He reached up to touch the helmet, to make sure it was real. "Like it has no weight."

"Believe me, it has plenty of weight," Mr. J. Ar said. "You might not be able to feel it, but the enemy will."

"Awesome," Levi said.

After putting on his helmet, Evan began strutting around, trying to act all warrior-like. Xavier put his on and stood straight and tall, like a soldier ready for battle. He gave Evan a shove to make him stop strutting.

Ivy put on her helmet, feeling the sides and top to make sure it was really there. "Comfy," she said. She flung her head down and up again, but the helmet did not budge from her head. "No straps either."

There was one helmet leftover.

"The final helmet is for Brianna," said Ruwach, taking the last piece of armor from the air and handing it to Levi. "It will be your job to see that she puts it on."

Levi swallowed hard and nodded, taking the helmet in two hands. "Okay," he said.

"This will help you." From his sleeve, Ruwach produced a small scroll made of delicate paper and sealed with the Crest of Ahoratos. He handed it to Levi. "Make sure she reads it."

Levi nodded, tucking the scroll in his pocket.

"He always has something up his sleeve," Evan mumbled.

"Now," Ruwach said, folding his long arms together, "Levi, Manuel, Xavier, and Ivy will return to earth with Mr. J. Ar to protect your friends and convince Brianna to release the Sypher."

Evan perked up, realizing his name hadn't been mentioned.

"What about me?"

Ruwach's whole being turned to face Evan; for a moment, Evan thought he could see two eyes glowing from the depths of the hood.

"I have a different assignment for you, Prince Evan."

CHAPTER 25

The Quaritan

Evan looked worriedly at his brother and his friends. *Here it comes,* he thought. *Ru knows I took the key. I'm gonna get it. He's going to throw me into a pit or something. Probably with alligators. Or lions. Or maybe he'll send me to Skot'os. After all, that's where Rook ended up.* But it wasn't Ruwach that put Rook in Skot'os, Evan reminded himself, after he had raced through several more horrifying scenarios. That had been Rook's choice.

"There is a quaritan in need of you." Ruwach's voice was surprisingly mellow.

"A what?" Evan muttered.

"There is only one way to capture the Ents, and that is to open a quaritan. A quaritan can be found and opened only by a Prince Warrior. And this one is assigned to you. You must find the right one and open it in order to capture all the enemy forces and close the portal."

"But . . . why me?" Evan asked, backing away from Ruwach, his eyes darting to his friends. "I mean, I'm the youngest here. . . . I'm not the smartest. And I don't even know what a—a quarreler—is! Why don't you send Manuel? He's way smarter. Or Xavier, he's stronger. . . ."

"Because I am sending you," Ruwach said. "You are the one for this job, Prince Evan. The only one."

Evan looked at Xavier, hoping he would speak up, tell Ruwach that he would go in Evan's place. Isn't that what big brothers were for?

"You can do it, Van," Xavier said instead, moving to him and placing a hand on his shoulder. "Ruwach believes you can do this, and so do I." He paused, as if his words surprised even himself. "In fact, if Ruwach says you can do it, you're the *only* one able to. Capeesh?"

"But I need—"

"You have everything you need," Xavier said. "Right, Ru?"

Ruwach nodded.

Evan looked around to the others, who were all silent, staring at him. He felt his heart bounce around in his chest. "Well, I'll try," he choked out. Then he heard a noise, like wind whistling through a tunnel, and turned in time to see The Book, on its golden pedestal, speeding toward him. But he didn't run for cover like the first time; nor did the others. They all waited for The Book to come to a screeching halt in their midst and hover, glowing radiantly.

Ruwach raised his arms, and The Book opened. Then he began moving his arms back and forth as if he were conducting an orchestra, a stream of musical notes filling the air as the pages flipped in time to the motion of his arms. When Ruwach stopped conducting, the pages stopped flipping. He raised up one hand, and the words lifted from the page, floating and rearranging in the air as they had done before.

Tear down strongholds.

Take. Captives.

Ruwach let the instructions glimmer in the air a long moment before pulling the words down and flinging them into each of the kids' breastplates. They felt the impact of the words inside themselves, warming their hearts, preparing them.

"What's a stronghold?" Evan asked, squinting at the word.

"It is the enemy's fortress built on wickedness and deception," Ruwach answered. "It must be torn down, demolished."

"Like the Fortress of Cháos," Xavier said thoughtfully. "Was that a stronghold? And didn't we already tear that down?"

"Precisely," said Ruwach. "Strongholds can be torn down, but they can also be rebuilt. Again and again. And if Ponéros cannot lure you to his stronghold, he'll try to build one *inside* of you."

"What? He can build a fortress *inside* of people?" Xavier asked.

"Yes. So that you'll be his captive even if you are not in Skot'os." Ruwach looked at the faces of his Warriors, each one lined with worry. "Do not be afraid. Your helmet will protect you from the strongholds of Skot'os *and* the ones he wants to build in you. It will keep you safe. Be prepared to use the shield as well—with that you can protect yourself and your friends. Your breastplate will give you guidance and protection. Your boots will give you a firm foundation. And your belt will hold everything together."

"But what about me?" said Evan, folding his arms over his chest. "How's it going to help me? I'm going to be all alone here."

"You are never alone, Prince Evan," Ruwach answered. "I am here to guide you. And the Words of the Source are in your heart." Ruwach reached out and placed one glowing hand on Evan's head. Instantly Evan felt the peace of those words sink into his brain, spreading through his whole body. He let out a breath and nodded slowly.

"Okay, let's do this thing," he said.

———

Evan found himself back in the place they'd started, the canyon with the colorful swirling sand walls. Except he was all alone in Ahoratos for the first time. He'd never been completely alone before. It felt strange and scary.

He turned slowly in a circle, trying to get his bearings. In the canyon it was hard to tell which way was up. Bright shafts of light filtered in from patches of sky above, but there didn't seem to be any obvious path to follow.

Which way?

Evan checked his breastplate and whispered under his breath: "Lead me."

Evan's breastplate began to blink. He turned to face one direction, but the breastplate blinked more rapidly. He kept turning until the light became steady. Straight ahead of him, a light shone between two red and orange walls of sand. Evan took a deep breath and put one foot forward, headed toward the light.

CHAPTER 26

The Birthday Present

Levi stood before Brianna's front door, two wrapped gifts in his hands. He'd been standing there almost two whole minutes, trying to get up the courage to ring the doorbell. *This is it.* He took a breath and pushed the button.

In a moment the door opened; Grandpa Tony stood in the doorway.

"Hey, Levi, long time no see," he said. He looked worn-out and worried. He opened the door wide so Levi could come in.

"How are you, Grandpa Tony?" Levi said. Everyone called Brianna's grandparents Nana and Grandpa. It was just the way it was.

"Okay, I guess."

"How's Nana Lily?"

Grandpa Tony closed the door. "Same. Doc says it's going to be awhile before we know. I came home for a few hours to see Breeny on her birthday. You here to see her too, I suppose?"

"Yeah."

"She's just sitting out on the swings in the backyard. Can't get her to come in and open her birthday presents."

"We were waiting for her at the Rec, but she didn't show."

"Yeah, I know." Grandpa Tony shook his head sadly. "She's so upset about her nana. But I think it's something more than that." He paused suddenly as if lost in thought.

"Like what?" said Levi.

"Oh . . . sorry. I was just remembering that I had something to show her in the attic, but we never did get around to that. . . ." He didn't speak for a while, and Levi began to get worried that Grandpa had forgotten he was still standing there.

"Uh . . . Grandpa Tony?" Levi stepped closer and waved his hand around to get his attention.

Grandpa suddenly looked down at Levi and shook his head. "What? Oh. Never mind about that. I got a call from the principal this morning. She failed a math test. Just doesn't seem to care anymore. Maybe you can talk to her."

He led Levi to the back of the house, where Brianna sat on a swing, dragging her toes on the ground as she rocked forward and backward. Fall leaves skittered over her feet, but she didn't seem to notice. He walked across the lawn toward her, looking around for any Ents that might be watching, or any Syphers, although he wasn't even sure what a Sypher would look like.

"Hey, Bean," he said, taking a seat on a swing next to her, his eyes still searching the trees.

"What are you doing here?" Brianna's voice was dull. She didn't look at him.

"I came to wish you a happy birthday. And give you a present."

"Oh?" Brianna glanced at him. "I thought everyone forgot about my birthday."

"I didn't. Here."

Levi handed Brianna the two gifts. She looked at them, shrugged, looked away.

"I don't want any presents. I just want Nana Lily to come home."

"Yeah, I know. I do too. But it's still your birthday. Besides, these aren't just from me. Open them."

Brianna shrugged, took the first gift and tore off the paper, revealing a scroll sealed with the Crest of Ahoratos. She broke the seal, rolled it open, and read the contents.

Take. Captives.

"Is this supposed to be a birthday card?" Brianna said sarcastically. "Take *what* captive?"

"This will help. Open it." Levi offered her the other box. A thin spray of light peered out from underneath the lid as soon as Brianna took it from Levi's hands.

"What is this?" said Brianna with a sarcastic laugh. "A disco ball?" She lifted the lid. A shimmering light kept her from seeing what was inside at first. She peered in the box, squinting.

"It's a gift from Ruwach, Bean. It's your helmet," said Levi. Brianna stared while Levi reached in. When he put his hands on the round shape it solidified, becoming tangible and real. He handed it to Brianna. "He told me to bring it to you. You need to put it on."

Brianna reached out to take the helmet.

Don't do it. It's a trick.

Brianna hesitated, her hands still in the air. The back of her neck started to itch terribly. A voice screeched in her mind.

It's a lie. It's a trick. Don't put it on!

Brianna's hands dropped to her lap, the scroll falling to the ground. The voice stopped screeching. The itching stopped too. She breathed easier.

"Thanks, but I don't want it." She handed the box back to Levi and jumped off the swing.

"What do you mean? Bean, this is going to help you. . . ."

"I don't need help. I'm fine. Just leave me alone." She ran toward the house, slamming the back door. Levi slumped, shaking his head in despair and looking down at the rejected gift. How was he ever going to get her to put the helmet on?

He reached down to grab the scroll before it blew away. And that's when something else caught his eye, something pink and sparkly. He bent over to see what it was—Brianna's lip gloss. Her favorite glitter gloss, which she was never without. She'd dropped it and forgotten it. Levi picked it up, thinking he would go back to the house to return it to her. But then he changed his mind and tucked the tube of lip gloss in his own pocket. For safekeeping, he thought.

He got up, still holding the gift box, and walked slowly back to his own house.

Brianna stood alone in the living room, watching through the window as Levi walked down the sidewalk, holding the box and the scroll. She felt a deep pit opening in her heart, like the feeling you get when your best friend moves away or your dog dies. Something vital was missing. And she didn't know how to get it back.

Stella appeared, flitting about before her, twinkling merrily.

You did the right thing. You don't need him. You don't need Ruwach or anybody. No one can help you. No one is going to make Nana Lily better. They're all telling you lies.

"He came to help me," Brianna whispered. "Maybe he *does* care about me."

Ha! What does he know about your troubles? Nothing.

That was true, Brianna thought. Levi's mom and dad were wonderful people who were both healthy and always there for him. He couldn't possibly know what it felt like to be abandoned by your own mother and then to have the person you most loved in the world get sick and maybe even die. Levi was an only child; he didn't know what it was like to have three older sisters who took up all the space in the bedroom and most of the attention. He didn't know what it felt like to feel . . . forgotten.

Brianna started to cry, softly.

Don't worry, I'll take care of you, Stella whispered. *Everything will be all right, you'll see.*

Outside the window, a large butterfly landed on a shrub and folded its gray, metal wings. Brianna didn't see it; she had turned away to wipe her tears. The butterfly's red eyes beamed through the window to Stella, who nodded her small head and beamed back in a special rhythm, sending a message.

Yes. It's time.

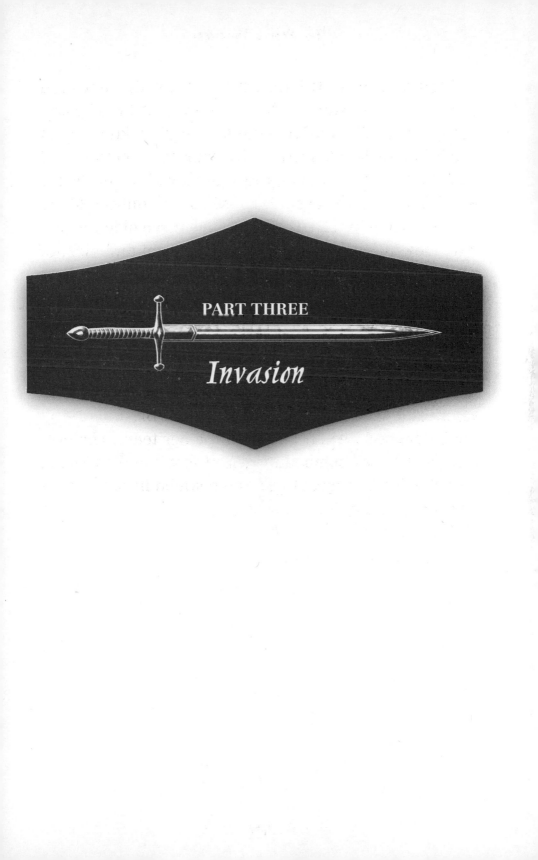

PART THREE

Invasion

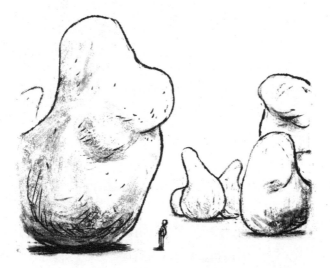

CHAPTER 27

Swarm

Rook, in full armor, sword slung at his side, entered the Corridor of Keys just as Ruwach was opening the empty box with the purple satin lining.

"How's Finn?" Rook asked casually.

"Making progress," said Ruwach, his voice steady and affirming. "But he is not yet battle ready. The Warriors will be few for the coming invasion."

Rook came up beside Ruwach and looked down at the box.

"Evan still has it?" Rook said with a sigh. "The key?"

"Yes. He is on a mission, to open a quaritan."

"Alone?"

"Not alone. I will watch over him. And *you* will protect him."

"Is that why I'm here?" Rook asked.

"You, more than anyone, understand the threat Evan faces."

"Does the enemy know Evan has the key?"

"He will as soon as Evan enters the Quaritan Field. Therefore, you must make sure Evan is not delayed or captured."

"Where is Evan now?" Rook asked.

"In the Sand Canyon."

Rook looked thoughtful. "There hasn't been a Prince Warrior to open a quaritan in many years. Are you sure Evan can do it?"

"He was chosen for the task; therefore he, in fact, is the only one fit to do it."

———

Ahoratos—The Quaritan Field
3:57 PM

Evan's footsteps got slower and slower. He was tired. How long had he been walking? It was hard to know. Time was so strange here in Ahoratos. Along with everything else. He wanted to stop and lean against a wall or sit on one of the weird sand formations to rest, but he didn't dare for fear it would collapse on top of him. He thought back to his first trip to Ahoratos, when he and Brianna had to walk down a dark city street with all the scary, crooked buildings that looked as though they would topple over any second. Which they did. Evan kept moving, not sure how long these sandy walls would hold up before that happened again.

He kept following the light of his breastplate, turning when it told him to turn. It was strange that even when there didn't seem to be a way forward, if he took a step in the direction the breastplate pointed, an opening would suddenly appear. It was there all along, he just couldn't see it until he got close enough.

But the sand-walls with their brilliant colors and outlandish shapes were starting to make him feel dizzy and disoriented. For all he knew he could be walking upside down. *Follow the armor*, he told himself over and over. He had learned from his previous journeys here that as long as he followed the armor, he would stay on the right track, even if everything around him went wrong.

A sudden fierce wind came up, nearly knocking Evan backward. He bent over, shutting his eyes and dipping his head against the billows of sand assaulting him. He suddenly remembered Levi and Brianna's first entrance into Ahoratos and the sand grobel that had attacked them—was this wind a sign that the grobel was coming again? Evan hoped not. But at least he had the seed to protect him this time. He dug into his pocket for his seed, just in case he'd need it. It was there.

He felt the key there as well.

He pulled it out and looked at it. The key. He'd almost forgotten he had it. He should have put it back before he left. Now he was headed into strange, new territory with the very key Ponéros had wanted so badly—the one Ruwach had only recently retrieved. This couldn't be good. It was terrible, in fact. He was in deep, deep trouble. Worse even than when he'd taken a ten-dollar bill off Mom's dresser that one time. Mom knew it, of course—that whole eyes-in-the-back-of-her-head thing. Did that mean that Ruwach knew about the key as well? Was this mission his way of teaching Evan a lesson he wouldn't forget?

Evan kept going, dipping his head against the furious wind. With every step, he felt as though he were pushing against some sort of gravitational force that was trying to knock him back. But his boots felt sure and stable, keeping him planted solidly on the hard ground.

Gradually the wind died down, as if realizing it was not going to be able to stop Evan from moving forward. He noticed the Sand Canyon walls were disappearing, like they'd been blown away, revealing odd-shaped rock formations as big as houses scattered over a barren landscape.

Evan gazed at the huge rocks, wondering if one of them was the—what did Ruwach call it? Quarter? Quaritan?—the thing he was supposed to open. It had started to get dark, the golden sky above him warring with the churning red-black horizon.

Skot'os.

Evan felt a rush of fear in his stomach. He must be pretty near the edge of Skot'os, where Forgers and Ents and Ponéros himself could be lurking around any one of these big boulders. In the sky, the huge skypods loomed larger and lower here than they had before. There was not a tree or a blade of grass to be seen. The whole world felt barren and cold and desolate. Like walking on the moon. He wondered again if Ruwach was trying to punish him for his disobedience. Or if his disobedience had led him to this place, a place from which he might never escape.

Evan felt a warmth in the center of his chest and looked down—the orb was spinning, glowing. He stopped walking and waited as it began churning words out into the air before him:

You know the plans I have for you.

Plans to help you, not to harm you.

The words seemed like an answer to his own thoughts. His fears. No, Ruwach did not mean him harm. This was a comfort to his churning stomach. He would be okay, somehow.

He didn't remember Ruwach ever placing that particular instruction in his orb. So where had it come from?

As he studied the words hovering before him, he realized that he *had* seen them somewhere before. This had been one of the unscrambled messages he'd received on his phone back on earth. So that meant that those instructions were *also* embedded in his breastplate.

Evan had often wondered where the instructions that appeared on his phone actually came from. It began to dawn on him that they might come from the same place as the instructions Ruwach gave him in the Cave: The Book. So even when he wasn't in Ahoratos, he was still able to receive instructions from the Source.

And encouragement. And hope. He smiled to himself, thinking of that.

He started to move forward again. Glancing up, he noticed that the two sides of the sky, the dark red and gold, were moving in a circle, like opposite streams of water coming together to form a whirlpool. He stopped and stared, shocked by the churning sky. It continued to twist and turn, color against color, layer against layer, until each one blurred into the other. But it was the center of the circular pattern that concerned Evan the most. It looked very dark, like a hole was forming, widening as it grew. A storm was coming—did it actually rain in Ahoratos too? He had never thought of that.

But as Evan watched, a mass of dark specks burst through the hole, spiraling toward the ground like a tornado touching down, pulsing with thousands of tiny red lights.

Evan realized this was not an ordinary cyclone. And it only took a moment before he knew for sure what it was.

Ents.

Hundreds. Thousands. Gajillions. The biggest swarm he'd ever imagined.

And they were headed straight for him.

CHAPTER 28

Ent–Nado

Rec Center
3:57 PM

While Evan walked through the Quaritan Field in Ahoratos, Brianna sat outside on the bench against the rec center wall, watching the kids play. She could see Levi at the skate park with his friends. Ivy was skating too. Since when did Ivy know how to skateboard? That really annoyed Brianna. Because, of course, Ivy was pretty good at it. Along with everything else that was so perfect about her.

Levi probably likes her better than you.

Brianna rubbed the back of her neck as the tiny, flutey voice repeated those words over and over. She knew it was true. Since that day on the swings, Levi hadn't bothered talking to her again. Now it looked to Brianna as if he'd found a new friend.

Well, fine. I don't need you anyway. I hate skate-boarding, she thought to herself.

On the other side of the field she saw Xavier playing basketball with a group of other kids. He hadn't even asked her if she wanted to play this time, like he usually did.

You don't belong here anymore. You need to find some new friends.

New friends? Maybe she *did* need to find new friends. She looked from group to group: the hopscotchers, the skateboarders, the kickball players. They looked pretty content by themselves. She turned and peered in the window of the rec center. Manuel was there, showing a group of elementary school kids how to make tinsel float using static electricity from his hair. The kids were completely enthralled by his demonstration. It looked sort of interesting to Brianna.

Don't go in there. That stuff's just for little kids.

Brianna's neck tickled again. Yeah, that was kind of dumb. Manuel was such a nerd anyway.

"Hey, Brianna."

Brianna looked up to see Miss Stanton standing in the doorway, a coffee cup in her hand, as always.

"Hi," Brianna said listlessly.

"How's your grandmother?"

Brianna shrugged. "She's still in the hospital. She can't talk. She's . . ." Brianna felt tears filling her eyes. She shut them to make them stop.

"I'm sorry about that." Miss Stanton sounded nicer than usual. She smiled awkwardly. "You want to help me with the beading craft? I know you're an expert at things like that. And, well, it's not really my thing."

Was Miss Stanton actually asking her to help with a craft? Because she was an expert? Brianna felt a smile creep across her face and a burst of excitement flutter in her chest.

She probably just wants you to babysit the little kids so she can spend the time texting her friends.

Brianna's smile ebbed away.

Besides, those kids are going to make a mess with all those beads. You'll spend half your time cleaning up after them.

Brianna turned away from Miss Stanton and shrugged. "I don't think so."

Miss Stanton sighed. "Well, okay, suit yourself." She went back into the center.

Your friends don't really like you. You're too bossy. If you were more like Ivy, you'd have lots of friends. If you were prettier, or nicer, or smarter. . . .

Brianna thrust her hands over her ears, trying to shut out that voice. Once it had been sweet as honey, but now it was like nails on a chalkboard.

"Stop!" she shrieked.

But the voice didn't stop.

"Stop!"

Levi heard the cry and stopped skating. He looked over to the center, where Brianna sat hunched on a bench outside the back door, her hands over her ears. He was certain it was Brianna who had cried that word aloud. How had he heard her, from so far away?

He kicked up his board. He needed to go talk to her again. Maybe now she'd listen to him. He reached into his pocket, fingering the lip gloss. He needed to give it back to her anyway. She hadn't had it for days, and yet she didn't seem to miss it at all. That was weird. Brianna never used to go anywhere without her signature glitter lip gloss.

He was about halfway to Brianna when the ground under his feet started to rumble. Levi looked down and saw that the blacktop was vibrating. And then something burst forth, an explosion of dust and rocks and—*something*—like a geyser at Yellowstone Park.

Levi jumped back, dropping his skateboard. He couldn't have known that this was happening at the precise moment that Evan was seeing those warring colors in the sky over Ahoratos.

From out of the hole in the ground came a stream of blackness, swirling in a vortex like a lasso being whipped in circles. It took a moment for Levi to understand what the blackness was.

Ents.

A mass of Ents, spewing forth from under the earth. They made a horrific noise, an earsplitting buzz like a squadron of amped-up killer bees, as they spiraled up into the sky. There they began to gather, forming a dense black cloud, hanging ominously over the playground.

Levi looked around—the other kids were still skateboarding, still playing their games on the playground, unaware of the danger at hand. Apparently, they could neither see nor hear what was happening.

The unseen invasion had begun.

Ivy skated hurriedly up to Levi and jumped off her board. "Let's go. We need to get your dad."

Levi nodded mutely.

They ran toward the rec center. Manuel had come out, still holding the PVC pipe he was using to make static electricity. He straightened his glasses for a better look.

"Could be an example of spontaneous eruption," Manuel said, "due to a buildup of CO_2 underground. . . ."

"Or a buildup of Ents," said Ivy.

"An Ent-nado!" cried Levi.

Xavier ran up to them, out of breath. "There's another one." He pointed to the basketball court, where another Ent-nado had erupted, this swarm rising up to join the other one that hung above them, blotting out the sun. A great shadow fell over the playground. Still, none of the other children seemed to notice. "We need to hurry."

The kids raced into the building. Levi stopped, noticing Brianna still sitting on the bench by the door with her hands over her ears. She didn't seem aware of what was going on.

"Bean!" Levi said, shaking her. "You need to get inside, now!"

She looked up at him, annoyed. "What for?"

"Open your eyes, look! Can't you see it? Can't you *hear* it?" Levi pointed to the Ents. Brianna looked, her eyes widened. Her mouth dropped open. Before she could speak, he grabbed her hand and pulled her off the bench and through the door.

The center was filled with kids doing homework and other activities. Miss Stanton, supervising the beading craft with a group of younger kids, looked exasperated. None of them could hear the growing rumble or see the erupting spirals of Ents outside the window.

"It's just like my dream . . ." Brianna said softly, still staring outside.

Mr. J. Ar came out of his office. He was already wearing armor, although it was glowing, translucent, as if not really there at all. No one could see it except for the Prince Warriors.

Mr. J. Ar gazed outside, a frown carved on his face. A third geyser of Ents had already erupted in another part of the playground.

"This way," he said, his normally booming voice very low and measured. He walked purposefully toward his office. Xavier, Manuel, Ivy, and Levi followed on his heels, but Brianna hung back, still mesmerized by the sight.

"In here," Mr. J. Ar said, rifling through his keys to open a locked door at one end of the room. The label on the door said "Storage."

Mr. J. Ar went in, followed by the rest. There were shelves with office and cleaning supplies. And against one wall sat a big old steamer trunk, so dusty it looked as though it hadn't been opened in a long time, the brass lock plate rusty with disuse.

"Whoa," said Xavier. "Is that—?"

"That's the trunk we just saw in the Cave!" Levi exclaimed. "I've been in this closet a million times, and I've never seen it before."

"It is always here when we need it," Mr. J. Ar replied. He opened the lid, releasing a torrent of dust and ethereal light that bathed the children in an unexpected peace in the midst of the current crisis.

The kids quickly pulled out their belts, boots, and breastplates and started putting them on. The armor was luminous and see-through, just like Mr. J. Ar's. Despite their urgency, they couldn't help but marvel at the way the transparent armor looked on them, moving like it was part of their own bodies. The boots locked around their legs, perfectly smooth except for the vents around their ankles. The belts blazed with the word *TRUTH*.

"It's like a hologram," said Manuel. "But it's real!"

"Can the other kids see this?" Levi asked.

"Some might," said Mr. J. Ar. "Other Warriors. But the enemy most certainly will. Don't forget the helmets. They will protect your minds from the schemes of the enemy."

Each of the kids grabbed a helmet and put it on; the helmets sealed around their heads, ears, and necks.

"Okay, let's go!" said Ivy, eager to go to battle against the Ents.

Mr. J. Ar pulled Brianna's helmet from the trunk. He held it out for Levi. "Now's the time."

Levi shook his head. "I tried before. She wouldn't take it."

"Try again. She won't be able to dispel the Sypher without the helmet."

"Do you want me to do it?" said Ivy, stepping forward.

"No," Levi said firmly, reaching forward to take the helmet from his father's hands. "I'll do it."

Mr. J. Ar gave Levi a small smile then turned to the others. "You all have your shields?"

Ivy reached in her pocket to show him her seed, which was already glowing. The boys did the same. Clearly the seeds were primed and ready, as they had been the last time the warriors had needed them.

"What about Evan?" Xavier said. "Is he okay? I mean, how do we know—"

"Trust Ruwach," Mr. J. Ar said. "You have your job to do, and Evan has his. Are you ready?"

The warriors looked at each other silently. They nodded. It was time.

Time for war.

The orbs of their breastplates spun in unison, churning out words that hung in the air before them.

Two words, stark and simple.

Fear not.

CHAPTER 29

No Fear

Fear Not.

Evan almost hadn't even noticed the simple phrase that had churned out of his breastplate. He quickly pulled his seed out of his pocket. It had turned bright red like it was on fire. He raised it up in his fist, deploying the shield. Thousands of red seed-lights spun around him just as the swarm of Ents descended. Their hair-curling shrieks, although muffled by the shield, pierced his very soul. Evan fell to one knee, bowing his head so he wouldn't have to look upon the ugly metal butterflies shooting their stingers at him. He didn't know what to do. He couldn't see to move forward; he couldn't go anywhere at all.

The minutes passed, and Evan's shoulder began to hurt from holding his arm stretched out for so long. He lowered it to ease the ache, but the shield dome around him became smaller, and the ferocious bugs drew closer than ever. There seemed to be no end to the flying storm.

"Help!" he called out. "I can't hold them off! My arm is . . . too weak. . . ."

But mine isn't.

It was Ru's voice, filling his whole mind. He looked up. Searching.

At that moment a brilliant flash cut through the swarm of Ents that bore down on him. Evan was shocked to see Rook appear before him, slashing a long, gleaming sword through the dense swarm, slicing and scattering the Ents, turning them to dust.

Rook glanced down at Evan only for a moment. "Get going! I got your back!"

"Rook?" Evan said, shocked. "How did you—?"

"Go, go, *go!*" Rook shouted.

Indeed, there was no time for conversation. Evan dashed forward, still holding his seed high enough that the shield covered him. He felt strength return to his body along with hope that maybe he would get out of this in one piece after all.

You know the plans I have for you . . . to help you, not to harm you.

He tossed those words in his head over and over as he plunged forward, keeping his attention focused on the steady beam of light from his breastplate. He glanced back from time to time at Rook, who leaped and twirled like a ninja warrior as he fought to keep the Ent swarm at bay, his sword swaying and dancing like a beam of light. *Gotta get me one of those things,* Evan thought fleetingly. He kept running as fast as his short legs would carry him, nimbly traversing the rocky ground and skirting the giant, lumpy boulders. Still, he could see no opening in any of them, no gap that would indicate a cave or an entry. Was one of these boulders the quaritan he was supposed to open? And if so, how was he to know which one?

He reached one of the rocks and began pounding on it, hoping a secret door might open. Nothing happened. He hurried to another one, running his hands over the surface, looking for a crack, a depression, something that would indicate there was a way inside. But all the boulders he encountered were solid. He tried kicking them as well, remembering how his boots had once turned a Forger into metal dust. But his boot made no impression in the solid rock.

Evan turned back to Rook, who was too busy swatting Ents to notice Evan's problem. He realized he'd have to figure this out by himself. There was no one else to ask.

Something small and bright flashed across his vision. Evan blinked. It looked almost like—a Spark. From the Cave. What was it doing out here? Then there was another one, as if the single Spark had split into two. Then four. Then eight. They continued to multiply, a shimmering curtain of lights dancing before him.

"What are you guys doing?" Evan asked, exasperated. Then the Sparks changed formation, creating a line with their light, a path through the field of giant rocks. Evan could have shouted with joy, but instead he just grinned, thrilled to see the trail they were laying out before him.

He started to run, following the twinkling path the Sparks had created, his boots fairly flying over the hard, barren ground. The path led toward another of the large boulders, this one slightly reddish in color with a very pitted surface. It was huge—as big as Evan's whole house. Was this the quaritan he was supposed to open? And yet, as Evan got closer, he saw no door, no crack, no opening in the rock's surface.

The Sparks had led him to another solid rock.

"Hey! Ru! Somebody! Let me in!" Evan had to lower his shield so he could pound on the rock with both fists. Nothing happened. He turned around to see Rook close behind him, still fighting off Ents with shield and sword. Evan raised up his own shield again, to protect himself from the attacking Ents that might get through Rook's barricade. Yet there seemed to be more and more of them, closing around the two of them. And there wasn't anywhere they could go from here.

They were trapped.

CHAPTER 30

The Storm Gathers

Rec Center
4:07 PM

I'm going to sound the emergency alarm," Mr. J. Ar said to the others. "It's what we use for tornado warnings. While Mary and I are getting the others in the shelter, you kids spread out, cover all the windows and doors as best you can. Keep the enemy forces from getting inside. Got it?"

"Just . . . *us*?" said Manuel, looking at the other kids nervously.

"We can do it," said Xavier. "We have everything we need, right?"

"Yeah. We got this," said Ivy, standing straight. She seemed to be a different girl when she had her armor on—sure and strong, her timidity giving way to a firm confidence. Levi and Manuel straightened as well, their resolve returning.

Mr. J. Ar was impressed at how calm and brave they looked. They were real Warriors now. He went to a metal box on the wall of his office and unlocked it. He flipped a switch inside, and a deafening alarm began to sound. The kids covered their ears.

Mr. J. Ar left the office and spoke loudly to the kids in the center. "Attention everyone! We need you to proceed calmly and quietly to the storm shelter. Immediately! This is an emergency! Mary . . ."—he pointed to Miss Stanton, who was looking in confusion at the perfectly blue sky outside—"please, make sure everyone gets downstairs and stays there until I give the all clear. I'm going to round up the kids outside. Hurry!"

"But wait—what's going on?" Mary protested.

"Just do as I ask!" Mr. J. Ar barked. He had never raised his voice to Mary—she paled at his tone. She quickly hustled the kids toward the storm shelter door, so frightened she even forgot her latte.

Standing at the window, Xavier watched the spiraling ribbons of Ents ascending from the opened wounds in the earth. He made sure his helmet was on right and gripped the seed in his hand, trying to slow his breathing, preparing himself. They were going to have to keep the Ents out of the Rec until Evan was able to open the quaritan to capture them. This worried Xavier a bit. He had always been good at following directions—Evan, not so much.

His jaw tensed as he thought about Evan, his little brother, alone in Ahoratos. He hoped Evan was okay.

Xavier turned his attention back to the center; he saw that Miss Stanton was having a hard time getting the kids to go downstairs. She shouted and whined, but mostly they ignored her. Xavier, with one more anxious glance outside, left his post to help her. Miss Stanton smiled at him gratefully.

Levi ran to Brianna, who was still standing in the middle of the room, watching all the chaos unfold around her but doing nothing. He held the helmet out to her.

"Please, Bean, put this on. You have to!"

No, don't.

Brianna shook her head. "I'm not a Princess Warrior anymore. I'm never going back to Ahoratos. Ruwach doesn't care about me. None of you do!" She turned and ran for the doors, brushing past Ivy and pushing against the crowd of kids who were trying to get inside.

"No, Bean, don't!"

Levi had no choice but to follow her.

Ivy watched them go barreling out of the rec center doors, skirting around the Ent geysers. There were six of them now, funnels of Ents shooting up and amassing into one giant Ent cloud overhead, making it almost as dark as night. They were gathering for the assault, which would start any second now. She hoped Levi and Brianna would find a safe place to hide once that happened.

Then she remembered what Ruwach had told her. She glanced back at Xavier and Manuel. She'd be a lot safer if she stayed here, with them and with Mr. J. Ar. But her assignment was Brianna.

Suddenly, Ivy felt something new open up inside of her—the inexplicable strength she had only experienced in Ahoratos—and she knew what she had to do. So she, too, squeezed through the doors and ran out after Levi and Brianna.

"Hey!" Xavier called after her, but she didn't respond. She didn't even look back.

"So now it's just the two of us?" said Manuel to Xavier in a shaky voice. "We can't stop—that—" He pointed to the cloud of Ents that had begun a slow, massive descent toward the rec center.

"We're gonna have to," Xavier said.

——————

Mr. J. Ar was outside trying to round up the last of the children when he saw his son and Ivy running after Brianna toward the big beech tree that stood near the edge of the property. The beech tree was the favorite climbing tree at the Rec; its low curling branches and wide canopy made the inside of it into a kind of fort. Mr. J. Ar considered going after them and bringing all three back into the center. But he decided against it.

The tree would keep them hidden, sheltered from the attack, at least for a while.

Hang in there, Warriors, he thought to himself. *Use your armor.* Levi and Ivy would be okay as long as they remembered not to rely on their own strength but the strength of what Ruwach had given them. They had to use their armor. And keep their helmets on.

———

"Bean!"

Levi tripped over a branch and almost fell. He thought he'd lost her for good, but as he recovered he saw her just ahead of him, breaking into the canopy of the huge beech tree. Levi followed her in. It was even darker in the tree than it had been outside, but he could see Brianna, sitting against the wide trunk of the tree, turned away from him, her knees drawn up to her chest, her head buried in her arms. He heard a soft sob, like she was crying.

And then Levi saw something else really strange—a blinking light on the back of her neck. He heard a noise, a low, uneven humming, like when people are talking in another room but you can't quite understand what they're saying. The rhythm of the humming seemed to coincide with the blinking light on Brianna's neck. Mr. J. Ar had said she had a Sypher attached to her, but Levi couldn't see anything but the blinking. He crept closer for a better look. But Brianna whirled suddenly and faced him, her eyes unfocused and glazed, as if she couldn't quite see him.

"What are you doing?" she demanded.

"You've got something on your neck," he said. "It's a Sypher. . . ."

"A what?"

"A Sypher. You brought it back from the Garden of Red, didn't you?"

"I don't know what you are talking about," Brianna lied, folding her arms.

"Look, Bean, that thing may have looked like something really pretty and friendly, but it's not. You have to get it off of you and capture it. It builds the fortress of the enemy in your mind. It's twisting your thoughts, Bean! It's making you act this way."

Brianna looked at Levi with a perplexed expression. She had seen Ponéros's fortress. In Sko'tos. Across the chasm in Ahoratos. And she distinctly remembered it being destroyed by the Olethron they'd sent sailing back there. How could something that massive be created inside of her, in her mind?

"That's silly," she said. "Just go away, Levi. Leave me alone!"

Come with usssssssss.

The voice sizzled like hot metal thrust into cold water. Brianna looked around, wondering where it came from.

"Did you hear that?" she said.

"Hear what? Bean, the attack is about to start. We don't have much time—"

"Don't call me that. My name is not Bean."

"I'm sorry . . . Brianna. Please . . . put this on—"

Don't listen to him!

Brianna stood up, confused. Then she looked up and saw something she hadn't noticed trailing her until this very moment. Sitting on a large branch of the tree was an enormous Ent, made of gleaming metal. It was as big as a bald eagle, its large angular wings folded up. It bent its head, its red eyes boring into hers.

Listen to me. I am your friend.

CHAPTER 31

The Storm Descends

Rec Center
4:15 PM

Mr. J. Ar corralled the last of the kids inside the center and shut the doors just as the massive Ent cloud descended, coating the windows and shooting darts against the glass panes. Their shrieking cries reverberated right through the walls and made the light fixtures vibrate.

"Everyone to the storm shelter!" Mr. J. Ar continued to roar as the remaining kids, frightened by his urgency, headed toward the shelter door. The shelter's concrete walls were thick and strong, and the door was reinforced. Mr. J. Ar hoped it would withstand an Ent attack if their other defenses failed. At least for a while.

"You take the front windows. I'll take the back." Xavier gave orders to Manuel and then rushed over to the back windows as they began to crack from the pressure of the Ents. Xavier raised his seed in his fist, deploying his shield. Manuel raced over to the set of windows by the front door. He glanced at Xavier then copied his movement, his arm shaking as he thrust his fist out straight. He'd never actually done this before. He gasped as the shield deployed, sending a shiver like electricity down his arm. Then he smiled.

He was amazed that his seed-shield reached out to cover all the windows. The other two walls of the center only had doors—one led to the gym and the other to the office. Both those doors were closed tight. But that didn't mean the Ents wouldn't get through them eventually.

Xavier looked over at Manuel and nodded approvingly. "Good. Keep it steady."

"What about them?" said Mary Stanton from the storm shelter doorway, pointing to Manuel and Xavier. "Don't they have to come down too?" She'd been watching the two boys suspiciously for some time as she continued to herd children down the stairs. "What's really going on here, Mr. Arthur? There's no tornado. So what's the matter?"

"Trust me, Mary. I'll explain later. Right now we need to get you and the rest of the kids into the shelter." Mr. J. Ar spoke in a loud but calm voice as he gently herded Mary down the steps. Then he shut the door tightly, standing before it with his sword drawn.

Ahoratos—The Quaritan Field
4:17 PM

"Help me, Ru!" Evan called out. He flattened his back against the rock, keeping his shield up to protect himself from the flying darts of the Ents. For a split second, he worried that his shield might shatter under the pressure. But then he remembered how it had withstood the Olethron. He relaxed a bit. But still, neither he nor Rook had any way out.

He felt something hot at the center of his back and jumped away from the rock. Where he had been leaning, a small bright spot appeared in the center of the stone. A tiny hole, filled with a light that was shining from within. And the hole got bigger. Gradually, Evan saw that it was actually a flame, growing ever brighter, burning through the giant boulder in front of him. *Rocks can't catch fire*, Evan thought to himself. But this one did. The fire branched out into two trails in a circular pattern, carving a fiery circle in the rock with a dark, empty center. Like a . . . doorway.

Was he supposed to go *through* this ring of fire? Seriously?

He turned back to Rook, but he was so busy blocking the Ents he didn't even notice. Evan faced the flame in the rock again. It was the only way inside that he could see. So, he took a breath.

Here goes nothing, he thought. And then . . . *then* . . . he walked into the fire.

———

Rec Center
4:17 PM

"Fire!" Manuel yelled, pointing toward the front doors. The glass doors in the front and back of the rec center looked as though they were on fire, as if someone had thrown a burning torch against them. White flames shot into the air, igniting Ents, melting them instantly as others scrambled to escape. Neither the adults nor the kids inside the center could see that something, *someone*, was within the flames, standing like a sentinel in both doorways simultaneously, arms outstretched to block the Ents from getting through.

It was Ruwach.

In the fire.

———

Ahoratos—The Quaritan
4:17 PM

Evan hadn't seen anything in the fire either. But indeed, there it was—there *he* was, Ruwach, standing inside the fiery doorway of the quaritan, his unearthly hands holding the flame.

But Rook could see Ruwach's presence, barely visible. He moved closer to the fiery rock as the Ents began to retreat, fearful of being melted down, turned to ash. Rook lowered his sword and bent over, hands on knees, trying to catch his breath. "Thanks," he said, glancing up at Ruwach. "So—Evan's inside the quaritan now?"

"Yes," Ruwach said placidly from inside the fire. "But stay alert. This is far from over. Ponéros will not give up so easily. He cannot allow Evan to succeed." Ruwach paused. "He wants both the boy and the key."

"But what about the others? On earth? Aren't you going to help them?"

Ruwach's response rang with the splendor of omniscience and eternity. . . .

"I am already there."

Rec Center
4:18 PM

Xavier and Manuel gasped in horror when the front door of the Rec burst open. They were certain that the Ents had managed to break through the firewall on the doors. But it wasn't Ents. It was an old man with fuzzy white hair and beard, wearing the same glowing armor as Mr. J. Ar and carrying a real, albeit rather rusty, sword.

"I see I got here just in time," said the old man, leaning against the door to catch his breath.

"Tony!" Mr. J. Ar exclaimed, coming up to him. "How did you . . ."

"It's Ru. He made a way for me through the fire. And . . . my granddaughter is in trouble." He straightened up and held up his sword. "Had to rummage through the attic to find this. I haven't used this thing in a long time. I hope I haven't forgotten how."

"I'm sure you haven't," said Mr. J. Ar. "Fortify the doors that go into the gym. In case they get through the gym windows."

Grandpa Tony nodded, brimming with confidence. "I'm ready."

CHAPTER 32

Inside the Quaritan

Evan gazed around at the strange new place he'd entered. He had run through the fiery door and was now, somehow or other, *inside* the quaritan. The fire still blazed in the opening, but he was alone—Rook had not come with him. Evan assumed that Rook was still on the outside, battling Ents.

Evan looked around. From the light of his breastplate he could see the walls of the quaritan were very lumpy and sort of purply. It reminded him of something he'd seen before. . . .

A geode! Like the ones in Manuel's room. The inside of a geode was hollow and lined with crystals, even though from the outside it looked like an ordinary rock. So that's what a quaritan was—kind of like a gigantic geode.

Ruwach had told him that he had to unlock the quaritan. He looked around for something to unlock, like a door or a keyhole. He wondered if the key in his pocket would work—maybe that's why he was the one chosen for this mission. He reached in his pocket and pulled out the key. That funny shaped end was not like any key he had ever seen before.

He crept along the edges of the cave, searching for a lock that might fit the key. A secret door, an invisible door, like in the movies—that would be cool. He searched high and low, turning his body this way and that to shine the light of his armor so he could see better. Nothing but lumpy purple rocks reflected back to him.

"What am I looking for?" he asked aloud. As if in response, the orb on his breastplate began to spin, spilling instructions out before him:

Seek and you will find.

Evan sighed—that was not really helpful. He *was* seeking already. He did another walk around, examining the rock walls even more carefully, but still he saw no holes that would fit a key, no recessed areas that might be a hidden door, no special tiles in the floor that lit up or sank or did anything no matter how much he stomped on them with his boots.

He had another idea and took off his belt, tossing one end up toward the ceiling, hoping it would stick to something so he could climb up and see if there was something up high he could find—something his much taller brother could have done easily. But the belt just fell back down onto his head. He sighed, putting it back around his waist.

Evan got tired. He sank down to his knees, lowering his head. It was no use. He was never going to figure this out.

Seek and you will find. The words echoed in his mind. He wondered what was happening with his friends back home. Had the battle they were going to face started yet? If it had, that meant he didn't have a whole lot of time to open the quaritan. He had to do it, somehow or other. He got up and kept looking.

And then he noticed something that hadn't captured his attention before: a dark stone mixed in with the purple-y crystals. It was black and rounded with a flat surface. Not pointed and colorful like the crystals. A swirling design was etched into the stone, delicate silvery lines that glowed in the light of Evan's breastplate.

Evan got up and went for a closer look. He saw that the swirling lines on the stone looked something like . . . *writing*.

ת

Evan put the key back into his pocket and reached up to touch the stone; after some tugging, it came loose. It was the size and shape of a baseball and sort of heavy. It reminded him of the stones in Manuel's room. . . . What did he call them? Lodestones? Some weird name like that.

Then Evan remembered something about those stones. They were magnetic. Evan felt his heart skip a beat. Maybe this stone was magnetic! And maybe, just maybe, that had something to do with unlocking the quaritan! It was just a little clue, but it was all he had.

He stared at the design engraved on the stone. He didn't recognize the symbol, but it had a similar style to the funny-shaped א on the Crest. Which meant this symbol could be in that same language. So how was he supposed to know what it meant? Ruwach would know what it was, but he probably wouldn't tell. Ruwach seemed to prefer the Prince Warriors to figure things out for themselves.

Maybe Rook knew. He might even have opened one of these quaritans himself at one time. Rook seemed to know a lot of stuff. But he was outside. Evan looked up at the ceiling. Maybe if he shouted loud enough, Rook could hear him.

"Rook! Are you there? Can you hear me?"

No answer. But at least he had a clue.

Evan moved farther along the narrow cave, searching for black stones among the colorful crystals. He quickly found another black stone and held it next to the first one. He felt a pull, the two stones repelling away from each other. Just like real magnets. So these two stones didn't go together. He simply had to find the ones that did.

Evan kept searching and soon found several more round stones. It was like once he understood what he was looking for, they were just there. Everywhere. He plucked them from the walls one by one and set them on the ground together. He began to arrange them in some order. Most of them repelled each other, but eventually he found three that actually stuck together.

אמת

Was this a word? Evan had no idea. But he figured it had to mean *something*. Maybe if he found more pieces, it would be clearer what this was all about.

As he got to his feet to search for more stones, pebbles and debris began to fall on him. The crystals inside the quaritan trembled slightly; he had to steady himself to keep from falling.

Give me the key. . . .

The voice Evan heard crackled like radio static in his ear. He pressed his hands against his ears and felt the helmet on his head heat up, the warmth running down his neck. The space around him brightened—the helmet was lighting up. The rest of the words of that hideous voice were garbled, so he couldn't understand them. That was a good thing—he was certain he really didn't want to hear what it had to say.

With new urgency, Evan continued to search for the stones with the odd markings. He didn't know how many he needed, but he had a feeling that he and his friends were going to run out of time very soon.

In Ahoratos . . . and on earth.

CHAPTER 33

Under Cover

Ivy stood just at the edge of the canopy under the beech tree and deployed her shield to cover as much of the tree as she could, keeping the attacking Ents from getting inside. The sound of the Ents descending over the rec center was thankfully muffled by her shield.

She was worried. Levi wasn't having any luck getting Brianna to put on her helmet. The more he pleaded, the more she refused. Neither of them seemed to notice Ivy standing there watching. She wondered if she should try to help but decided Levi probably wouldn't want her interfering. Besides, she doubted she would have any more luck than he was having.

But then Brianna looked up, her attention caught by something in a tree branch overhead. Ivy and Levi both strained to see what Brianna was seeing. Ivy put a hand over her mouth so no one would hear her gasp of panic.

The biggest Ent she'd ever seen was perched in the crook of a tree branch. It made a rumbling noise, as if it were actually talking to Brianna. And she was listening.

"Bean . . . Brianna, can't you see what that is? It's an Ent!" Levi said urgently, trying to draw her attention away from the big bug.

Brianna didn't respond. She kept staring up at the Ent, her eyes unfocused. Like she was being hypnotized. Ivy saw that weird thing on the back of her neck blinking furiously.

Levi stepped forward, reaching out to put the helmet on Brianna's head. The large Ent shrieked, launching a dart. It hit Levi in the chest, and he stumbled backward—his breastplate repelled the dart, but the helmet flew from his hands and rolled away. Before Levi could grab it, the Ent shot another dart at him, which glanced off his helmet. Levi fell backward on the ground, dazed. Brianna continued to stare at the Ent as if she had no idea what had just happened.

"Bean, please," Levi cried, "get your helmet! Put it on! Before it's too late!"

Brianna shook her head.

The helmet rolled toward Ivy, stopping right before her boots.

Rec Center—Inside
4:25 PM

A bead of sweat trickled down Mr. J. Ar's brow. The swarm of Ents against the windows was so dense it blocked every bit of sunlight, shrouding the center in darkness. The Warriors had only the glow of their breastplates and the red lights of their shields to guide them. But the boys were struggling to cover all the windows by themselves. It was just a matter of time before . . .

"Help!" Manuel called out. One of the windows on his side had started to crack. "I can't hold it!"

"Stand firm, Manuel!" Mr. J. Ar ordered.

But Manuel took several steps backward, his shield wavering. The Ents took full advantage, breaking through the cracked window and sweeping into the rec center.

"Mr. J. Ar!" Manuel cried desperately, struggling to stop the onslaught by himself.

"Xavier! Manuel! Come to me!" Mr. J. Ar beckoned from the shelter door, where he was stationed.

Xavier and Manuel retreated from the windows to join Mr. J. Ar, their shields and helmets protecting them. The cloud of Ents made it hard for them to see where they were going.

"Stay in front of this door; form a shield wall!" Mr. J. Ar said, shouting to be heard over the screeching of the Ents and the shrill whistling of flying darts that turned everything they hit—books, backpacks, jackets—to solid metal.

The two boys nodded, standing together to form a glittering red shield wall in front of the shelter door. The swarm kept coming, pummeling their shields with their long, lethal darts, but the Warriors held fast.

"Stand firm!" Mr. J. Ar said again. Then he turned and nodded to Grandpa Tony, who was covering the gym entrance. Tony nodded back. He stepped away from the gym door and began slashing at the Ents with his sword, shattering whole swaths of them into dust. Mr. J. Ar did the same, his sword glowing brighter with each Ent it destroyed. Xavier and Manuel watched with wide eyes at the sight of so many Ents falling in defeat.

But still they came. More and more of them, streaming in through the broken windows.

"I don't know how much longer I can hold out my arm," said Manuel, struggling to keep his shield up.

"I'll help you," said Xavier. He reached with his free hand under Manuel's sagging elbow. Manuel let out a breath, relaxing slightly.

"Thanks." Then he murmured to himself: "Seven, eight, nine, ten . . ."

They waited.

And hoped for Evan to open the quaritan.

Soon.

CHAPTER 34

Here and There

More stones. More strange letters and designs. Evan raced to fit them together.

דבר נעים

The quaritan walls shook and trembled, dropping dust and pebbles on his head. He didn't feel them though; his helmet seemed to deflect not only the voice of the enemy but the impact of the falling debris as well. Yet the quaking was getting worse. He was running out of time.

He kept arranging the magnets, figuring out how they fit together.

Hurry, hurry, hurry! The message, or writing or whatever it was, still made no sense to him. He only hoped he was on the right track.

Rook stayed within the protection of Ruwach's fiery circle, his shield in one hand, his sword in the other.

The Ents couldn't reach him. But he noticed that the bulk of the swarm had moved to attacking the quaritan itself, their darts chipping away at the huge rock bit by bit. The enemy may not be able to get to Evan, but if he destroyed the quaritan before Evan could open it, the Ents would not be captured or contained.

And Evan might never get out.

Don't give up, Evan, Rook said to himself. *Don't. Give. Up.*

Ahoratos—Inside the Quaritan
4:29 PM

I can't do this.

Evan leaned back from his work and stared at the incomprehensible message taking shape from the magnets he had fit together. Even if he finished the puzzle, he still wouldn't know what it meant. If this message actually contained the secret of how to open the quaritan, he wouldn't be able to read it. He was tired. His fingers were scraped and sore. The shaking was coming more frequently now. Evan knew that the enemy was not happy with his progress. Sweat curled in his eyes—he could barely see what he was doing anymore.

"What's the use?" he said aloud. "I can't do this. It's too hard. I'm not smart enough."

His breastplate brightened, the orb spinning, churning out another message into the air before him:

Be strong and courageous.
Do not be discouraged.
Do not be afraid.

Another instruction he'd gotten days ago on his phone. He wished he'd paid more attention to it then. He would have been more prepared for this moment. But there was no time for wishing. Evan let the words sink deep into his heart. He sighed, rubbing dust from his eyes, straining to examine the remaining crystals despite the shaking. He kept working.

And finally, he was down to two. There were no more black stones in the quaritan that he could find. As he fit the first one into the puzzle, the entire quaritan rocked as if it had been knocked off its foundation. Evan fell sideways, the last stone flying from his hands. He struggled to right himself, covering his eyes to avoid the dust and debris falling all around him. He searched around with his hands—but that last piece of the puzzle was gone.

Desperately, Evan crawled along the rough floor, searching for the missing piece. It was hard to see anything at all, with all the dust in his eyes. He coughed and choked, struggling for breath. The shaking continued to worsen. He wanted more than anything to just give up, to find some way out of this awful mess. He wanted to go home.

But then he had an image in his mind of Brianna sitting by herself in the rec center, sad and alone. Something had gotten hold of her. That thing . . . that *Sypher*. He rose up, balling his fists in anger. His friend was in trouble. He remembered how she had stayed with him through the dark city on their first trip to Ahoratos. He couldn't abandon her now. He had to find that last stone.

He kept searching, combing through the rocks and pebbles and broken crystals that littered the floor of the quaritan. *Show me, show me where it is.* He whispered the words over and over, hoping Ruwach could hear him.

Then he remembered—the stone was magnetic. Maybe he could use one of the other stones to find it! He crawled over to the nearly completed puzzle and yanked off the last stone he had placed. Then he scanned it over the floor of the quaritan, using it to detect the stone he was missing. The rocks on the floor kept shifting as the trembling worsened, but Evan kept trying.

Finally, he felt something latch onto the rock in his hand—it had to be the missing piece!

Rec Center—Outside
4:30 PM

Brianna felt tears stinging her cheeks.

"Stella, where are you?" she said, ignoring Levi's pleas to put on her helmet.

I'm right here, silly.

Her neck tickled. For the first time she began to make the connection—the tickle on the back of her neck and . . . Stella? She was the one talking to her? Telling her all those things?

"It's lying to you," Levi said. "Whatever it says is a lie!" He tried to rise, but the Ent shot another dart at him. He fell backward again, dizzy and disoriented.

"Stella wouldn't lie to me. She loves me. . . ." Brianna barely whispered.

Levi spoke in breathless gasps: "It doesn't love you, Bean! It can't love you! It's just trying to control you! Your family loves you . . . and your friends . . . and . . . me. You need to put on the helmet. You need to hear the truth! Please . . ."

"Stop!" Brianna cried. She lowered her head, covering her ears so she wouldn't hear Levi's voice—or Stella's.

Ivy, still at the edge of the tree, watched in horror as the giant Ent on the branch rose up, spreading its enormous wings. She saw Levi still on the ground, too far away to help. The Ent let out a terrible screech, a braying cry of victory, and aimed its next dart directly at Brianna.

Ivy knew she had to do something. She picked up the helmet and ran toward Brianna.

"Watch out!"

Brianna looked up, confused. Ivy leaped in front of her, just as the deadly dart flew into her path. . . .

Ahoratos—Inside the Quaritan
4:30 PM

Evan quickly scrambled back to the puzzle, the two final stones in his hand, and placed them at the end of the puzzle.

אמת כבוד נעים בין בדברים האלה

And as he did, the shaking suddenly stopped. . . .

Rec Center—Outside
4:30 PM

. . . And so did the dart.

In the split-second moment when the dart was just about to hit Ivy . . .

It didn't.

Ivy could hear her own breathing—rapid and shallow. Her eyes, which had slammed shut to prepare for impact, opened to see that the dart had stopped in mid-air, inches in front of her. As if it had been frozen in the middle of space. Then it disintegrated, turning to dust and falling harmlessly to the ground.

Ivy gazed down at the dusting on the grass that had been an Ent dart a moment before. When she looked up again, the enormous Ent in the tangled branches began to shrivel up into a blackened shell that fell off the tree and landed in a pile of dust in front of them.

Ahoratos—Inside the Quaritan
4:31 PM

Evan waited, listening. There was no sound. But when he looked at the stones again, he saw that the designs etched into them were changing, transforming, the strange letters morphing into new shapes, radiating with their own inner light.

True. Honorable. Lovely.

Think on these things.

Evan realized he could read the words now. Then the entire puzzle lit up like it was set on fire, shooting out a wide, flat beam of light that burned through the quaritan's roof of crystals like a blowtorch cutting steel. Evan shielded his eyes from the blinding light. He could feel the intense heat waft toward him as the quaritan began to split apart.

Ahoratos—Outside the Quaritan
4:31 PM

Rook saw it happen—something he never thought he would see with his own eyes. The quaritan was opening like a clam. It made a tremendous noise, as if the whole land was about to erupt. The attacking Ents shrieked in alarm, for the inside of the quaritan was as bright as the sun, shooting up a twisting column of fire that spiraled upward for what seemed like miles. It spun feverishly, drawing the Ents into its vortex like moths to a flame. They were powerless against it.

"Evan!" Rook raced toward the quaritan, fearful that Evan, too, would be consumed by the towering column of fire. But Ruwach, standing before the opening quaritan, held up an arm to stop him.

"I've got him." Ruwach's other arm pointed to the sky. Rook looked up, seeing nothing at first but the fiery tornado. Then something large and fast streaked by overhead, scattering the roving swarm of Ents that still lingered there. At first Rook thought it was an enormous Ent. He raised his sword, as if in defense. But then he heard a noise like a trumpet turned inside out, and he started to laugh.

Tannyn swooped into the fiery quaritan and disappeared. Rook sucked in a breath, holding it in anticipation until Tannyn finally shot back out of the firenado with Evan secured in his huge jaws. They looked unharmed. The dragon soared into the sky, tossing Evan onto his back, and then dove for the ground. He landed badly, as usual. But Rook could see that Evan was smiling.

"You did it," Rook said, looking up at Evan with a big smile. "Good job."

Evan, exhausted and covered in dust, bent over to give the dragon a pat on his scaly hide. "Thanks, old buddy," he whispered.

Tannyn craned his neck around to give Evan a toothy grin. "Gorp."

Rec Center—Outside
4:33 PM

Ivy held Brianna's helmet out to her.

"Here, Brianna. Put this on. Please."

Brianna stared at the helmet a long time. Finally, she took it and slowly put it on her head. The helmet flickered then lit up as if it were powering on. Each of the tiny facets twinkled, spraying the tree branches with twirling lights. There was a piercing squeal, like a runaway train trying to stop. Something flashed around Brianna's head, and she jumped, nearly falling backward. Ivy reached out to steady her.

"Hey, are you okay?" Ivy asked.

Brianna blinked several times, shaking her head.

"I think so—"

A pitying cry rose up from the ground at Brianna's feet. She looked down to see a tiny winged creature lying in the dirt, its once silvery wings shriveling up, just like the big Ent's, until it was nothing but a jumble of blackened wires.

"It's the Sypher," Ivy said, nearly breathless. "It's dead."

"Stella?" Brianna said, staring down at it. Then she looked up at Ivy, her eyes soft, like she might cry.

Ivy smiled at her. "Welcome back."

Brianna turned to look at Levi, who had risen and was moving toward her slowly, one hand over his breastplate. He looked like he was in pain. But he was smiling.

"You okay now, Bean?"

"I'm . . . fine," Brianna murmured.

She looked once more at the mangled wires that had once been her friend. Then she heard a new voice in her ear, clear as a bell, sweet and soft, a voice filled with music and love:

True. Honorable. Lovely. Think on these things.

Rec Center—Inside
4:33 PM

"What's happening?" Xavier shouted.

Something *was* happening. The swarm of Ents that had engulfed the center appeared to be lifting, relieving the pressure on his and Manuel's shields. Mr. J. Ar and Grandpa Tony stopped swinging their swords, gazing in awe as the massive cloud of Ents was sucked out of the rec center through the broken windows. The horrible insects screamed in terror as some unseen force suctioned them back toward the holes in the ground outside.

Both boys retracted their shields and ran to the windows to watch as the black spinning swarms went down into the holes, which sealed up as if they had never been there at all.

Ahoratos—Outside the Quaritan
4:33 PM

The sky above Ahoratos split apart, revealing a dark hole from which a twisting black cloud descended, plummeting toward the firenado that raged from the opened quaritan.

"What is that?" Evan shouted as he slid from Tannyn's back.

"The Ent swarm, from earth," Rook said. "The quaritan is trapping them."

Before long Evan could see the Ents, shrieking and fluttering furiously, unable to get away from the irresistible force of the quaritan.

"It's like your leaf vacuum," Evan said aloud.

Rook laughed. "Yeah, a little bit like that."

The quaritan itself trembled and roared as it captured the Ents, like a monster swallowing a flock of birds. Then it began to close, two jaws snapping together, making the ground under Evan's feet shudder. It sealed up just as the last of the Ents, still shrieking their skin-prickling cries, disappeared inside.

Then all was quiet, like every bit of sound had been sucked into the rock along with the Ents. Evan took a deep breath, relaxing. It was over. The Ents were trapped inside the quaritan, and it was sealed.

"Is that it?" Evan asked, hoping he'd been fast enough to help his friends.

"Not quite," said Rook. "Wait for it."

The quaritan started to quake as if all the Ents inside were trying to escape. It rocked this way and that, breaking away from the ground with more deafening rumbles. Evan and Rook were swept off their feet by the shaking; Tannyn cried out "Gorp!" and hunkered down, lowering his head to the ground. Finally, the entire boulder broke away from the ground and lifted into the red-gold sky, floating toward the other large lumpy objects that hovered there.

And that's when Evan realized what it was.

"A . . . skypod?" he said aloud. "That's what those things are?"

"Very good, Evan," said a deep voice. Evan turned around to see Ruwach standing behind him, his arms folded into his sleeves.

"Ru!" Evan said. "Where've you been?"

"Here . . . and there." Ruwach made a noise that Evan thought might have been laughter, but he couldn't be sure.

———

Rec Center—Inside
4:34 PM

Grandpa Tony charged through the back door, carrying his sword as he ran out onto the playing field, toward the beech tree.

He didn't have to go far. He stopped when he saw Brianna emerge from under the tree with Levi at her side. They were both smiling. Brianna saw her grandfather and flew into his arms, laughing and crying at the same time.

"Grandpa, I'm so sorry—" Brianna backed away suddenly, staring in wonder at her grandfather. His armor. And his sword.

"Grandpa—are you—?"

Grandpa Tony chuckled. "I was going to tell you all about it," he said. "But that was when you didn't want to—"

"Help you clean the attic," Brianna said, lowering her gaze. "I'm sorry, Grandpa. . . ."

"Thank you, Levi. You're a good friend. And a fine Prince Warrior."

"Um . . . Ivy helped too," Levi said, pointing to Ivy, who was standing a few feet away.

Grandpa glanced at Ivy and smiled. "Thank you, *Princess* Ivy."

Ivy grinned. Mr. J. Ar and the other boys gathered around them, high-fiving each other, celebrating their victory and Brianna's return.

"Mr. Arthur? Is it okay to come out now?" Mr. J. Ar turned to see Mary Stanton standing in the doorway, looking around curiously. "Is it—over?"

Mr. J. Ar turned to her and smiled. "Yep," he said. "It's over. Tell the kids it's safe to come out."

Ahoratos—Outside the Quaritan
4:34 PM

"Is that all of them?" Evan asked, glancing up at the newest skypod floating in the red-gold sky. "Are they all gone now? For good?"

"No, not all," Ruwach said. "There are many more. And more quaritans to hold them."

Evan felt disappointed. "So what's the point then? If we can't ever destroy them completely—"

"Prince Evan. You win a war battle by battle. You keep pressing on. *That* is victory."

"But couldn't the Source have won this battle all by himself? Why did *I* need to open the quaritan?"

Ruwach was silent a long moment. Then he spoke quietly, almost tenderly: "That is the wrong question, Prince Evan. The question is not why did the Source *need* you to open it, but why did the Source *want* you to open it."

"Okay then. Why did the Source want me?"

"The Source is not only in control of all things but how all things are accomplished. Yes, He could have done this alone. But then you would never know what could be accomplished *through* you, young Warrior."

Evan thought about this. "So, that's why He doesn't just fix everything here and on earth? That's why He doesn't win our battles for us?"

Ruwach's hood nodded slowly. "His ways are mysterious. You may not always understand them. But there is one thing the Source does want you to understand with all your heart: through Him all things are possible. Even the most difficult things."

Evan once more thought he glimpsed a pair of glowing eyes deep within Ruwach's hood. Something about that made Evan feel bigger and braver and . . . safe. But it did something else too—it made him want to be better. To get rid of any hidden things weighing him down. To tell the whole truth.

He reached into his pocket and pulled out the key.

"I took this," he said, holding his hand open so Ruwach could see. "It was wrong. I'm sorry."

Evan noticed that Ruwach wasn't shocked or alarmed. In that moment, he was certain that the guide had known all along.

Ruwach reached out with his glowing hand and gently plucked the key from Evan's open palm. One of his shining fingers touched the edge of Evan's hand. And with the touch, an unexpected peace swept over Evan, like a cool breeze on a hot summer's day. He closed his eyes and breathed deeply. Evan knew, even though Ruwach hadn't said any words, that he'd been forgiven.

"I will see that it is returned to its proper place," the little guide said, his hand disappearing once more in his sleeve. "Remember, Evan, it is *never* too late to make things right."

"That's for sure," said Rook with a laugh.

"However," Ruwach went on in a different tone, "you broke the rules of this realm and, for that, there are consequences."

"What consequences?" said Evan.

Ruwach didn't answer. Instead, he let that word drape over Evan like a heavy blanket: *consequences*. Evan didn't know exactly what they would be, but he was pretty certain they would not be good.

CHAPTER 35

Homecoming

A large banner, made from a bedsheet, was hung across the front porch of Brianna's house, with "Welcome home, Nana Lily!" written in purple glitter paint. In the cool of the evening, Brianna's sisters and her friends Levi, Xavier, Evan, and Manuel stood underneath the banner, shouting and cheering as Grandpa Tony's battered old station wagon pulled up in front. Mr. J. Ar, who had driven the kids over to welcome Brianna's grandmother home from the hospital, stood to one side, his arms folded over his broad chest, a huge smile on his face.

The three sisters ran down to the car, shrieking happily. Grandpa Tony emerged from the driver's seat, waving his arms to get them to calm down.

"Hold up, hold up! Let's not get too excited, okay? Don't want to give her a relapse now. Winter, Crystal, get the wheelchair out of the back."

Brianna jumped out of the backseat—Grandpa Tony had given her the honor of accompanying him to the hospital to pick up her nana. She waved to her friends and then opened the passenger-side door excitedly.

Her sisters pulled the wheelchair out of the trunk and rolled it over while Grandpa Tony and Brianna helped Nana Lily out of the car. She had trouble moving one side of her body, but the other side was ready for action.

"Stop fussing already! I'm just fine, I tell you!" she said, waving the help away. Her voice sounded funny, like she was having trouble pronouncing all the words correctly. "Doctor says I need to do for myself if I want to get better." Once she was settled in her wheelchair, she relaxed, looking up at her granddaughters and smiling. "Thank you, girls. You're gems."

"I'm so glad you're back, Nana," said Crystal, hugging her. Winter and Nikki took their turns hugging her too.

Nana Lily nodded, lifting her good arm to wave slightly. "It's good to be home."

Brianna nodded, tears filling her eyes. "Can I push you?"

"Go right ahead," said Nana Lily.

Brianna reached around to the handles and started to push her grandmother proudly up the sidewalk to the house. Her friends gathered around to greet Nana Lily, everyone talking at once.

"Bean," said Levi, "look." He pointed behind her. Brianna turned around to see Ivy standing under the streetlight, holding a small bouquet of flowers. Ivy walked up to Nana Lily and held out her offering.

"Hi, I'm Ivy," she said. "I live down the street—I heard you were coming home today, so I brought you these."

"How lovely!" said Nana Lily.

Brianna looked at Ivy, surprised at her new confidence. She didn't seem at all like the shy girl she'd known before.

"They're lilies," Ivy said. "Because of your name . . ."

"Lilies! Of course. Well, come in, come in. Perhaps we have some cookies—"

"I made a cake!" said Crystal.

"Uh . . . sure," said Ivy, eyeing Brianna carefully.

"Cake? I want some cake!" shouted Evan.

They all began talking while Mr. J. Ar and the boys picked up the wheelchair and carried it up the steps to the house. Brianna hesitated, turning to look at Ivy.

"I'm sorry," she said. "About the way I acted toward you. I don't know what got into me. Well, actually, I *do* know what got into me. But anyway, I'm sorry."

"It's fine. Actually, it's better than fine. Ruwach knew exactly what we both needed."

Brianna looked at her quizzically. Ivy realized that she'd have to explain. "Here's the thing. Ru gave me *you* as an assignment. He wanted me to make friends with you. I assumed it was because you needed something . . . that you needed *saving*." Ivy paused, searching for the right words. "But now I realize it wasn't just about saving you. It was also about saving *me*."

"Saving you?" Brianna tilted her head, confused.

"Yeah. It's strange, but in Ahoratos I could leap off a cliff without even thinking about it. There I have courage that, for some reason, I've never had here. In school, or at the Rec . . . I've always felt afraid. I can't even tell you how hard it was for me to talk to you the first time. But now I see I can do it. And so much more.

I can be brave. I can take risks. I can really, truly be who I was always meant to be. A Princess Warrior."

Brianna smiled. "Yeah, I get that." She turned to go up the steps, and Ivy followed. But then she stopped again, took off her headband, and turned to Ivy.

"Here," she said.

Ivy looked at the headband, uncertain. "What are you doing?"

"I'm giving you this. You said you liked it. You *did* like it, right?"

"Yeah, I did." Ivy blushed, taking the headband and putting it on. "How does it look?"

Brianna quickly opened the front door and flipped on the porch light so that she could get a better look. "Stellar," she said.

A butterfly fluttered past the girls, and Brianna ducked, covering her head and gasping a little. Ivy laughed. The butterfly landed on a flower near the front steps, batting its wings slowly.

"Is that what I think it is?" Brianna whispered.

"It's a butterfly. Just a regular old butterfly."

"You sure?"

Ivy nodded.

"Do you think it's—watching us?"

Ivy studied the butterfly for a moment, then shook her head. "Nope."

"Girls! You coming in or what?" Grandpa Tony peeked his head out of the door. "If you don't hurry, you'll be out here in the dark of night! And plus these boys are going to eat all the cake."

"Hey, we can't let that happen," Brianna said. She straightened, standing tall, like the Princess Warrior she still was. "Let's go."

Ivy nodded. The two girls charged toward the door, scaring the butterfly, which fluttered lazily away.

As Brianna walked into the house she was startled by Levi, who stood there as if he had been just about to come out.

"Oh . . . hey," Levi said. "I was—looking for you."

"For me?" Brianna said.

"I'll just go in," said Ivy with a smile. She moved through the door.

"Uh . . . Ivy?"

Ivy stopped and turned to Levi, wincing slightly as if she was afraid of what he might say.

"Yeah?"

"Thanks, for helping Bean . . . and me. I sort of— misjudged you, I guess. I'm sorry about that."

Ivy's mouth dropped open slightly. Then she smiled.

"No big deal," she murmured. She glanced at Brianna, grinned, then went into the house.

"What's up?" Brianna asked Levi. "Cake gone already?"

"No, I . . . I wanted to give you this." Levi pulled something out of his pocket and handed it to her.

"My lip gloss!" Brianna shrieked. "I was looking all over for it!" She took off the cap and smeared it over her lips, which soon shone with a fresh application of glitter.

"Now you really look like yourself again," Levi said with a smile.

"I feel like myself again," said Brianna. "Thank you, Levi. Thank you so much. For everything." She leaned toward him and gave him a glitter-filled kiss on the cheek.

Just then Evan came running toward the door. "Hey, Levi, where's the—" He stopped and stared at Levi, who stood frozen like a statue as if he'd lost the ability to move.

"What's that?" Evan said, pointing to Levi's cheek, which was stained with a lip-shaped glob of glitter. "Is that what I think it is?"

"Huh?" Levi finally moved, his hand reaching to his cheek.

"Evan!" Brianna said, stepping toward him. "I need to thank you too. For going into the quaritan all by yourself. That was really brave."

Evan backed away from her, suspicious. "Yeah, it was nothing."

"Nothing? Are you kidding? That was like the bravest thing I've ever heard of a kid—a Prince Warrior—doing."

"Well, I wasn't really alone. Ruwach was there. And so was Rook. . . ."

"Well, I thought it was incredibly brave," said Brianna.

"Really?"

"Really. In fact, I think you deserve a hug." She opened her arms and stepped toward him. Evan yelped and made a mad dash back into the house. Brianna burst into peals of laughter.

Levi just shook his head. "Girls," he said.

Brianna chased after Evan with her arms still open, laughing. She saw him dart into the kitchen and followed, stopping in her tracks when she got to the doorway. Her family and friends were gathered around the candlelit table, on which sat a large chocolate cake.

But the cake didn't say "Welcome Home, Nana." It said, "Happy Birthday, Brianna." Brianna stared at the cake, puzzled.

"We never did get around to having that birthday party we planned," said Grandpa Tony, standing beside Nana Lily's wheelchair.

"Well, that's okay," Brianna said. "You didn't have to. . . ."

"You mean you don't want your surprise?" said Nana Lily. She spoke slowly, but there was a mischievous sparkle in her eye.

"Surprise?" Brianna had almost forgotten about the surprise. She assumed, because of her behavior, that she didn't even deserve a birthday present. She thought of how she had thrown aside Levi's present—her helmet—so abruptly. It still made her wince to think about it.

"Close your eyes, and put out your hands," Grandpa Tony said.

Brianna looked around at all the faces—her sisters smiling with great anticipation, her friends trying hard not to laugh. She could barely breathe for the excitement she felt in her stomach. Maybe it was the hoverboard she wanted! Or new clothes? Her mind raced through all the possibilities.

"Close your eyes, silly!" Crystal cried. "Hurry!"

Brianna closed her eyes and held out her hands. She heard some shuffling and muffled giggles. Then something plopped into her arms. It wasn't heavy and hard like a hoverboard. It wasn't light and soft like clothes either. It was . . . squirmy. And fluffy.

"Open your eyes!" said Nana Lily.

Brianna opened her eyes and gazed into a small furry face with large, dark eyes. She opened her mouth and let out a shriek.

"A . . . puppy?!"

Everyone broke into cheers and laughter. The little animal recoiled at all the noise. It was black with a white patch on the top of its head. Brianna pulled it into her arms and buried her face in its fur. A puppy. Something—*someone*—all her own. She couldn't ever remember being as happy as she was at that moment.

"Thank you," she managed to say. "She's the sweetest thing I've ever seen."

The puppy whined and licked her face several times.

"It was my idea," said Nikki.

"Was not," said Crystal, elbowing her.

"You've got to take care of her yourself," Grandpa Tony said. "Feed her and train her and all. I'm sure your sisters will be glad to help."

"Sure, for a price," said Nikki with a laugh. "But it won't be much."

"I will, I will!" Brianna said.

"I'll help too!" Ivy said. "That is, if you want me to." Brianna smiled at her. Her friends gathered around to pet the puppy, all but Manuel.

"I'm rather allergic," he said with a sniffle.

"What are you going to name her?" Levi asked.

"I think I'll call her . . ." Brianna paused, gazing down at the white furry center of her puppy's forehead. She thought of Stella. That creature hadn't lived up to her name, but maybe this one would. "I'll call her Star," she announced, "in honor of this cute white patch. It kind of looks like one, I think." Brianna chuckled as the puppy burrowed into her arms as if she was planning to stay there a long, long time. "I always liked that name."

"Ah!" said Nana Lily. "That's perfect."

As if in approval, the night sky outside lit up with a million stars. And, from somewhere above them, Ruwach hovered, watching his Warriors and their loved ones celebrate this happy moment. He was proud of them, but he knew their journey was not yet finished. There would be struggle and challenge that would test them to their very core. But it would not come without victory and joy and hope.

Because they were, after all, Prince Warriors.

Epilogue

A sleek black dragon glided through the fog-filled sky on silent wings, headed for the enormous skypod that hovered over the blackened shell of what had once been the Fortress of Skot'os. The Forger on its back—a huge metal creature that looked more machine than man—guided it to a quiet landing and slid down.

This skypod was not like the others that dotted the sky over Ahoratos. For when the Forger's metal feet touched the surface, a crack appeared, widening to a trap door that led to a spiral staircase descending into the skypod's dark interior. The dragon let out a muffled growl as the Forger dropped through the hole and the door closed over him.

A moment later the Forger pushed through tall iron doors and entered the throne room, snakes hissing and slithering over his metal boots, annoyed by the disturbance. It approached the throne slowly, its iron-plated legs creaking, its footsteps like clanging cymbals in the vast space.

The twisted figures embedded in the massive throne began to moan, as if in terrible pain. The Forger stopped before the formless shadow that occupied the seat of the throne and bent to one knee with some difficulty.

You—failed? The voice of the shadow was low and searing, like a brand on flesh, and yet so loud it echoed throughout the room.

We could not stop them from opening the quaritan, lord. The Forger's voice was mechanical, without any modulation. *They had—help. The elders. The purple one—*

QUIET! No more excuses. We have lost an army—and a fortress—to a group of children. I will not tolerate this. They must be stopped.

They are Prince Warriors. They are stronger than we thought.

You are afraid of children now? The shadow laughed, a hideous sound. *Did you retrieve nothing?*

Only this. The Forger raised one mechanical arm and opened its fingers. In its metal hand there lay a small scrap of twisted metal.

They left this behind.

The scrap was charred black, except for one sharp edge that was stained red with blood. A few threads of clothing hung from the jagged tip.

It belongs to one of them, said the Forger, eager to please the master.

The shadow began to laugh, a hideous, echoing sound that made the faces in the throne moan piteously. Even the snakes slithered away in fear.

Aw. They left something behind, Ponéros said. *This will serve us well. Call the Weavers. There is work to do.*

To discover the
hidden secrets of The Prince Warriors, go to

www.theprincewarriors.com

FROM *NEW YORK TIMES* BEST-SELLING AUTHOR

PRISCILLA SHIRER

WITH GINA DETWILER

THE
PRINCE WARRIORS
AND THE
SWORDS OF RHEMA

III

Keep reading for a sneak peek at book 3 . . .

The Prince Warriors and the Swords of Rhema

Finn ran to the edge of the rocky precipice and skidded to a halt, sending a flurry of pebbles into the deep fog below. His heart beat like crazy in his chest. He couldn't look down without feeling dizzy. He panted hard, struggling for breath.

The narrow rock he stood on shook as the pounding footfalls of the Forgers closed in. Finn had no idea where he was now. But he knew he had nowhere to go.

Finn had been out exploring the land of Ahoratos, learning the ins and outs of being a Prince Warrior. After a life spent in the dark prison of Skot'os, the beauty and splendor offered on this side of Ahoratos nearly overwhelmed his senses. Forests with trees as tall as mountains, rivers and streams with water that sparkled like fine jewels, rolling hills choked with wildflowers of every imaginable color. Color itself was something wholly new to Finn, who had lived in a world of endless gray his entire life.

He was about to head back to the Cave when he'd heard a sound—like a cry for help—so pitiful and sad it nearly broke his heart. He'd heard that sound before, coming from his own mouth as he had sat in Ponéros's prison, losing all hope that he would ever get out. He ran toward the pathetic wail, which led him to a bridge that spanned a deep chasm.

He stopped, gazing at the pretty cobblestoned walkway with the ivy-covered railings. Was this the Bridge of Tears that separated Skot'os from the rest of Ahoratos, the one he had heard about when he was still a prisoner? He wasn't sure.

But then the cry came again. Finn drew nearer. As he did, he noticed that halfway across the bridge, the rustic cobblestones morphed into black steel girders that disappeared into a thick fog on the other side. He felt a chill run down his spine. *Skot'os must lie beyond that fog*, he thought. But he knew as long as he stayed on this side of the bridge, he would be safe.

Again the horrible cry of distress filled the air, and a figure emerged from the fog, limping toward Finn over the metal girders. He gasped—it looked like a prisoner of Skot'os. The figure was dragging one of his metal-encased legs behind him, obviously struggling, desperate to escape from that dark, malevolent place. Finn felt a rush of adrenaline—he had to help rescue this prisoner as he himself had been rescued! He had been hoping for an opportunity like this ever since he'd received his armor from Ruwach and begun learning the ways of the Prince Warriors.

Without thinking further, Finn ran over the bridge toward the prisoner, who looked at him pleadingly, whimpering, unable to speak any words.

"I'll help you!" Finn whispered. "Quickly! Come with me!"

Finn reached out to take hold of the prisoner's arm—but as soon as he did, he knew he'd made a mistake. The prisoner's half-human face darkened and hardened, his body lengthened, straightened, new plates of metal taking over the uneven patches of human flesh. The prisoner's human-looking eyes disappeared behind round red glowing discs. This was not a prisoner at all. It was a Forger.

Finn snatched his hand away and turned to run. The Forger grabbed for his shoulder, but Finn managed to evade him. He glanced back and saw that there were several more of them, charging out of the mist on the Skot'os side of the bridge. They'd lain in wait for him. It was a trap.

Finn was naturally pretty fast, and his boots made him feel as though he were flying over the cobblestones. But the Forgers' huge steps covered twice as much ground at the same time. Once off the bridge, Finn tried to run back to the Cave, but he wasn't sure of the way. And he was too busy fleeing Forgers to pay attention to the blinking light of his breastplate.

Now he regretted it. Somehow, he had made a wrong turn and ended up trapped on this narrow ledge, hovering over a seemingly bottomless pit. He skidded to a halt and heard the sound of pebbles cascading into the deep fog below. There was no escape.

His heart pounded. He struggled to breathe.

"Ruwach! Someone! Help me!" Finn cried aloud.

He got no reply.

The Forgers closed in on him, their metal hands reaching out to grab him. Finn knew he was done for. He would turn back into the half-metal prisoner he'd been before. No. He couldn't let that happen. He wasn't going back there again.

Then he remembered his shield. He pulled the tiny red seed out of his pocket and thrust his arm out before him. The shield burst forth from his tightly closed fist, a spray of brilliant red lights creating a dome of protection around him. The Forgers stopped in their tracks and roared, waving their metal arms around angrily.

Finn let out a breath of relief. He kept his arm straight out and tried to take a step forward, pushing back against the strength of the Forgers with his shield. But they appeared to be immovable. He tried again with no luck. He kept his arm erect but began to feel the pressure of the Forgers mounting as they closed in on him. Pushing. Pressing. He struggled to keep his shield deployed.

As he stood there, protected but still surrounded, he wondered what he should do. He felt the ground under his feet shift as he struggled to keep his footing.

He glanced down and saw a crack forming in the rock of the precipice. In a moment it would break off, and he would fall into the pit.

"Tell me what to do!" he called out, hoping Ruwach, wherever he was, could hear.

The orb of his breastplate began to spin, churning out words that hovered in the air before him.

Resist the enemy, and he will flee.

Finn remembered this instruction from The Book the last time he'd been with Ruwach in the Cave. That word rolled around in his mind.

Resist.

The only other time he'd heard about resistance was from his high school football coach during weight training. *"The heavier the resistance, the more muscle you will build. The stronger you will become!"* he had bellowed over the clank-clank sound of the heavy metal plates.

Resist the enemy, and he will flee.

Build strength.

Heavier. More muscle.

Finn steeled himself, gathering all his strength and focusing it on the arm that held the shield. This was all he could think to do. He opened his mouth and let out a thunderous growl as he pushed his shield into the Forgers with all his might. Then he took one step toward them.

Resist . . . resist . . .

He took another step, gasping for breath, every muscle in his body straining to the breaking point. He could feel the rock he stood on give way; he could hear the ominous cracking, the showering of pebbles as it began to break off. He kept his focus on his shield, moving, pushing, resisting.

His renewed resolve seemed to weaken the Forgers, for now they were inching backward, their heavy iron feet kicking up dust and dirt that lodged in their metal joints, causing them to stumble.

Resist!

The faltering of the Forgers gave Finn new energy, and he pushed harder and harder, leaping over the crack just as the rocky precipice broke free. He teetered on the edge of the chasm, throwing all his weight into the force of the shield. He thought his arm might break from the effort, but he kept it out straight, his fist clamped on the seed. He took another step. And another.

Resist.

Soon he was clear of the edge and gaining traction, pushing the now powerless and clumsy Forgers backward. A new plan formed in his mind. He sidestepped to the right so that the Forgers were forced to swivel with him. Now *they* were the ones with their backs to the precipice.

Finn let out a yell, a brawling victory cry as he thrust the Forgers steadily backward, his resistance as lethal to them as kryptonite to Superman. The Forgers howled as if in pain, waving their arms helplessly.

Finn was practically running now as he steered the Forgers right to the edge. With one last powerful thrust he sent them reeling over the cliff. He watched as all of them cascaded into the mist below, disappearing from view. He stood motionless for several seconds, shocked and paralyzed at the sound of their pitiful cries. As the noise subsided, Finn retracted his shield and stared out into the empty distance.

He closed his eyes and let out a long, long breath. It was over. He'd done it. He'd faced the Forgers and beaten them. But instead of pride, he felt an overwhelming sense of gratitude. Without the guidance of Ruwach, the instruction from the Source, and the power of the armor, he would never have prevailed.

"Well done, Prince Finn."

Finn whirled to see Ruwach standing behind him, his hands folded into the long sleeves of his purple robe, his face still invisible in the deep hood. Finn knelt at once, bowing his head. He always did this when Ruwach appeared to him; Ruwach had taken away his metal parts and made him whole again. Flesh, again. His only desire now was to serve Ruwach and the Source with all of his being.

Suddenly Finn noticed that Ruwach was not alone. The other Prince Warriors he'd met in the Cave walked up beside him, looking at Finn quizzically. They seemed surprised to find themselves here. With him.

"What happened?" said the tallest one, Xavier. Where'd those Forgers go?"

Finn pointed silently to the edge of the cliff.

"What . . . they just—went over?" said the youngest, Evan. He looked shocked.

"Did you throw them off?" said another kid, Levi.

Finn shrugged. "I just . . . resisted."

"You did indeed," said Ruwach. "They didn't antici-pate that you would."

"Who? The Forgers?"

Ruwach nodded. "They did not expect one so young or newly freed to know the secret power of resistance."

Finn lifted his head a little in a humble sort of pride.

"You were tested," Ruwach continued, "and now you have been strengthened by your resolve. You are ready now." He paused as if in thoughtful reflection. "In fact, you all are." He extended one of his long arms out to encompass the kids.

"Ready? For what?" said the girl named Brianna, tilting her head.

Ruwach's arm stretched up; his white glowing hand emerged from his sleeve, one long finger pointing toward something in the distance. Finn and the children all turned to look in that direction.

Ruwach was pointing to the tall mountain that stood at the very center of Ahoratos, the one that they'd marveled at before. Its peak was still invisible underneath a veil of clouds, but only for a moment. When Ruwach pointed, the clouds began to separate, pulling back like a curtain to reveal the top of the mountain fully for the first time. It was entirely flat, as if the tip had been cut off.

"Cool," whispered Ivy, the girl with the red hair. "A volcano."

"Possibly a fumarole," said the boy with the glasses, Manuel. "Although I've never seen anything quite like *that*."

A thick, white vapor, like steam, emanated from the flat peak of the mountain. It did look an awful lot like a volcano. Except different. For although the mountain appeared very still and calm, they could sense a movement within it, like the pulse of blood pumping through a vein. Somehow, the entire mountain seemed to rise and fall steadily. And they were certain that they could hear a soft wispy sound ascend from its flattened peak, each hushed exhale in cadence with the steady rhythm.

It was as if the mountain were . . . *breathing*.

"The Mountain of Rhema," Ruwach said. He spoke the words very quietly, as if even he were awed by them. "The mountain awakens when it is time."

"Time for what?" Xavier stepped forward, his eyes glued to Ruwach.

"Time for you to receive your swords."

Acknowledgments

With extreme gratitude to . . .

. . . my incredible ministry partners at B&H Publishing Group. Dan, Michelle, Rachel, and Jana, I am so extremely grateful for your investment in this work. Thank you for prioritizing this story and these characters. It's an honor to equip the next generation of Warriors with you.

. . . the creative genius of Gina Detwiler. Collaborating with you on this manuscript has been a joy. This story could not have been as rich and thrilling without your input. Your creativity astounds me, and your dedication inspires me. Thank you for the gift of your skilled pen. It has helped me to put this book into the hands of young readers everywhere.

. . . Lois Elizabeth Farris, the newest Princess Warrior in our family. God's got big plans for you, sweet girl.

. . . Jerry Shirer—You are the inspiration for Mr. J. Ar. He's the embodiment of maturity and strength in this series, and that is exactly what you are to me. Thank you for being a provider, visionary, friend, husband, and champion for me. Most of all, thank you for being a warrior—a Prince Warrior.

. . . Jackson and Jude—Your father and I have great expectations for you. The journey of faith that the Lord has planned for you will be epic. We are praying that you will be strong and courageous followers—Prince Warriors—who will take the risk and go with God. I can tell you with all assurance that it will be worth it.

. . . my father, Dr. Tony Evans, and my grandfathers, James Basil Cannings and Sherman Arthur Evans. The adult male figures in these stories are named after you. Your choices and faithfulness have shaped the trajectory of our lives. Your life and legacy live on in us—your children, grandchildren, and great-grandchildren.

About the Authors

Priscilla Shirer is a homemade cinnamon-roll baker, Bible teacher, and best-selling author who didn't know her books (*The Resolution for Women* and *Fervent*) were on *The New York Times* Best Seller list until somebody else told her. Because who has time to check such things while raising three rapidly growing sons? When she and Jerry, her husband of sixteen years, are not busy leading Going Beyond Ministries, they spend most of their time cleaning up after and trying to satisfy the appetites of these guys. And that is what first drove Priscilla to dream up this fictional story about the very un-fictional topic of spiritual warfare—to help raise up a new generation of Prince Warriors under her roof. And under yours.

Gina Detwiler was planning to be a teacher but switched to writing so she wouldn't have to get up so early in the morning. She's written a couple of books in various genres (*Avalon* and *Hammer of God*, under the name Gina Miani) and dramas published by Lillenas and Drama Ministry, but she prefers writing (and reading) books for young people. She lives in Buffalo, New York, where it snows a lot, with her husband and three beautiful daughters. She is honored and grateful to be able to work with Priscilla on The Prince Warriors series.

Don't miss any of the adventures from this action-packed series!

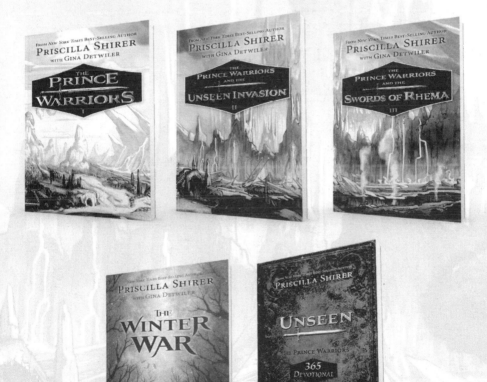